D1128691

# The Little Rogue in Our Flesh

# THE LITTLE ROGUE IN OUR FLESH

## Yves Navarre

Translated by Donald Watson

Quartet Books
London New York

First published in Great Britain by
Quartet Books Limited 1989
A member of the Namara Group
27/29 Goodge Street, London W1P 1FD

Copyright © 1977 by Editions Robert Laffont, S.A.
Translation copyright © 1989 by Donald Watson

British Library Cataloguing in Publication Data

Navarre, Yves, *1940–*
    The little rogue in our flesh
    I. Title   II. Le petit galopin de nos corps.
    *English*
843′.914 [F]

ISBN 0-7043-2725-2

Typeset by AKM Associates (UK) Ltd, Southall
Printed and bound in Great Britain by
BPCC Hazell Books Ltd
Member of BPCC Ltd
Aylesbury, Bucks, England

*The Little Rogue in Our Flesh*

# First letter from Joseph

Saint-Pardom, 20 June 1899

Dear Roland,
How beautiful it was on the road this morning before dawn. I
listened to my own footsteps. And kept one ear open for yours.
Distance has created an intimacy between us. Here back in this
house which my mother no longer rules, as if death had made a
clean sweep and removed all traces of human life, I find it vital
now to express to you the utter tranquillity of my feelings, the
serenity of my pain and how everything within me crystallizes
around your presence. In this letter I wish to take my time with
time, take time with everything, and above all beg you never to
efface within you any part of what we are. Letters like hearts can
be torn to pieces. Every heart has its dungeons. Forgive these
metaphors. I know you dislike them.

I suppose I must, by way of preamble, report the funeral to you.
Know then that it was all hustled through yesterday very early in
the morning in a side-chapel of the Cathedral of Saint-Pierre. Dr
Rigand, or I should say my father, sent a very fine wreath, the
finest; there was only the one. Red roses set in a garland of dark,
sharp-pointed leaves. One of those wreaths that prick you. My
mother had no love for cut flowers. So to the very last gesture
Rigand knew how to humiliate the woman who had remained a
stranger to us, such was the blame heaped upon her for her guilt in
producing a natural son: myself.

1

There was a great gathering. Five of us. The *curé* of Castelneau – for the arch-priest had declined to officiate, using the early hour as an excuse – the caretaker of the cemetery, two acolytes to bear the coffin and the writer of this letter. Oh, and I was forgetting someone: you! Lurking in the depths of my being. You may smile at what I am about to tell you: every day the feeling I have for you modifies my conduct. Listen.

So there was my mother, a woman who neither would nor could do anything throughout her life but conceal me, laid out in a box with no handles or decoration, just as she had wished. A simple resting place for a sweet-faced woman whose very last look will have been denied me. The Father Superior had failed to inform me till the following afternoon. As he explained, he wanted to 'break the sad news' at eventide, then and not before. What tact! What affectation! Ah, these priests distort everything. Thus it was difficult for me by night to make my way to our good old town, to cover those seventeen leagues we know so well, with all their crossroads and detours, our little valleys and those curving hilltops you so often like to compare to the sprawling bodies of women. Oh no, I wasn't 'sad'. I wanted to see my mother one last time, as though for the first. That's all.

At Larressingle I jumped out of a rickety cart to catch Antoine Surrelac on his way home after an evening with his Belle Jezebel. He recognized me. And we were off at full tilt in his tilbury. At least thirty times I thought we would tip over in the ditch. A full moon. And as he whipped his two Arab steeds along he never stopped singing. I did not announce the news of my bereavement. He set me down before the gates of Saint-Pardom. Then for the first and only time he spoke to me. In an over-loud voice he said: 'You're not going to let the black crows get you, are you? You, a creeping Jesus? Not on your life!' And he drove off laughing.

When I entered the drawing room they had already nailed the coffin down. The *curé* of Castelneau had sat through the night with Noellie, to watch over my mother. He simply said: 'It was so

2

hot. We couldn't wait. It's this morning.' And that was it, dear Roland. The coffin looked very small to me. I had to be satisfied to imagine my mother inside. Noellie had already packed her bags. She has gone back home to Tressens. Without waiting. She never even came to the Mass. Or the cemetery. She asked me for the shawl over the piano. As a memento. But nothing more. And above all, no wages. 'You don't ask the dead for money,' she fired at me as she held out a deformed old hand, knotted like a vine stock. A domestic hand. And then goodbye. She wouldn't even let me carry her suitcase to the gate, where her son was waiting. He didn't dare come in. At daylight a hot wind blew up.

'Creeping Jesus . . .' 'It's this morning . . .' 'Ask the dead for money . . .' How surprising other people's words can be. As if the outside world was suddenly impinging on me and confronting me with its weird verbal rites. When they spoke to me they all smiled. Surrelac's old conqueror's smile, that old gallant like a dashing musketeer. What style! And the beatific smile of the *curé* as he turned to face the coffin to say the words of the Requiem. Yes indeed, may she rest in peace at last, poor woman, she knew how to keep faith with the place where she lived out her life and her passion. Is that a cause for sarcasm and beatitude? And then that other cutting edge of Noellie's smile. Like a tit-for-tat for so many years spent in the service of a woman at whom the town had pointed the finger of scorn and who had no longer dared to show her face outside. Are the gates of Saint-Pardom as heavy as that?

As if prisons were not enough, human beings have perfected the art of creating purgatories. What is punishment for some confers virtue on others. This has finally convinced me of one thing: I shall not take my vows. Me, a creeping Jesus? I want to live my life. I therefore have the audacity to tell you that I am waiting for you. I, Joseph. Your friend. Our world is topsy-turvy, isn't it? All those insistent signals you sent out as an adolescent. Those first letters of yours which I never answered. Those notes you slipped under my pillow in the dormitory at college. I pretended I never found them. All those poems you used to write to girls, when I knew then as I know now that they were and still are addressed to me. So many years spent together, so much shared but unspoken affection.

I suppose keeping quiet was my way of sounding you out. Doubtless I wished to reach that moment of self-abandonment when our whole being is under distraint. When we admit the inadmissible. When we forget the shallow morality that condemns those who love each other and tries to separate the two that make one. This morning my footsteps were yours. I heard mine as if they were yours. We were together. Wearing the same pair of studded boots. Smile, my friend!

I was six years old when I saw you for the first time. School had just started again. The first thing you said to me was: 'I'm six and a half!' And a half! Ahead of me? You will receive this letter on my birthday. Twenty-two! Joseph is twenty-two. He has come back home. And you, Roland, a winter's child, you are twenty-two . . . and a half! And about to take your degree in politics! In Paris! Two seasons separate us. And I, the summer's child, was so enthralled by you that I said nothing. And you, the winter's child, how good it is to recall it again, how good and yet how galling, you said everything to me that I should have said to you. You will always be two seasons ahead of me.

It was a short Mass. It is important, this account of it. For I shall never mention this event in my life again. The caretaker of the cemetery and his two acolytes bore the coffin on ropes. The *curé* of Castelneau said it was too early to toll the bell. And I followed the hearse with its white box and its red wreath through our empty silent town. Closed shutters everywhere. To say goodbye to my mother, our town slept late that morning. And what a terrible clatter they made at that hour, the wheels of a ramshackle cart slowly grinding over the paving-stones of the Grand-Place, the Promenade and the Boulevard de Gesles. Now you understand. We passed in front of Rigand's house. I signalled them to halt. I took the wreath. The *curé* wanted to stop me. 'Don't, Joseph!' I laid the wreath on the steps of my father's house. I returned to my father the tribute he was paying my mother. It was only natural . . .

A small coffin. A tiny little coffin! A doll's funeral. And my name, my mother's name, engraved in large letters in the stone of the family vault: TERREFORT. Dark shadows inside. All those black boxes. And now that I am writing to you my sentences collapse and disintegrate. I need a new language to speak to you. What kind of language? What happened that morning seemed to me so ceremonial, boring almost, that only now do I feel some emotion in describing it.

Castelneau rushed off in a pique, curtly requesting me to convey his respects to the Superior of the College. I offered a few coins to the caretaker and his acolytes, then I remained alone in front of the vault, turned towards my mother with my back to the town. So many staring eyes behind the shutters and the blinds! When, taking the same route back, I reached the Boulevard de Gesles, the funeral wreath had gone from Rigand's steps.

That was it, Roland. In vain I left the gate wide open yesterday. Nobody came. I did not really want any visitors anyway. I merely wished to be sure that nobody would come. I spent my day drifting from room to room, discovering this house that I never really knew, having been practically forbidden to stay here during the first twenty-two years of my life. This house that you do not know either, it being so inconceivable that you should visit the mother of someone who in fact had no existence. Someone who, rescued by our holy Fathers, would in his turn become a holy Father. The wearing of a cassock banishes many a sin from the minds of the people of our town. So they wanted to erase me from the world to which I have returned this morning. May this letter tattoo its marks on both of us. Some moments in one's life are inscribed in indelible ink. And the way some eyes look at you can never be effaced.

To think that we were taught to count not with marbles but tallow-candles!

And if that bell had been tolled, it would have reminded me of you. Of your father climbing up the bell-tower of the Cathedral of Saint-Pierre, on the day of the plebiscite for the young Napoleon III, only to find himself arrested, brought to justice, sentenced and deported to Cayenne for ringing out the death-knell. Something else to bind us, profoundly united as we already are. Your father and my mother, two scapegraces through whom we have already paid the price for being what we are. And we shall never stop becoming what we are.

Yes, I am at Saint-Pardom. Any day now you will be at Copeyne. *We* shall be here. In our town. Together. I shall go where thou art. Thou shalt come where I am. Perhaps your Copeyne will become the country retreat for my Saint-Pardom. The winters in one place, the summers in the other. You see, I tell you everything. I am making tremendous plans for the future. In this single letter I am answering all the messages you sent me from Paris, messages which the Father Superior instructed me not to answer and which deep down I forbade myself to respond to, so firm was my wish that you should detach and free yourself from me, so disturbed was I by our affinity. But at the turn of this new century, is there the promise of anything stronger? And how long will it last?

Believe me, our future is still to be recorded. When we disappear, everything will still be in the making. We have a lifetime in front of us in which to crack the riddle, pierce the meaning of each and every moment. Complete understanding is unobtainable. Incompletion is what I propose. I owe the idea to you. You were always suggesting it to me.

Take a good look at Paris the Overpowering and come back to me soon. Come back to us! For the last time draw up your inventory of codes and modes. Walk off with your diploma, find a secure post, no matter what the income so long as it provides you with

6

independence. Come back to where you *are*: the inventory here is inexhaustible. Never have the evening breezes demanded so insistently to see us both again. Never have the waters of the Verse and the Gesles so carefully combed out their weeds, inviting a windswept pilgrimage. Never has the grass grown so thick and so tender. Never has the stonework of our town smelt more strongly of grain and of straw, of sunshine and of you. Everything defers to us in welcome. The Father Superior was right to wait till eventide in his attempt to touch me with the news. It was you who really let me in: through our secret way out, the door behind the vestry that we only used while the nettles were waiting to be cleared. This long letter gives everything away. So that nothing is given up. I have never known ink to be so clear or my pen to be so frank. This reply has been brewing inside me far too long for me not to go on to the point when we were starting to feel, I writing to you and you reading my words, curiously confused and ready for anything.

Remember in the *Aeneid* that line from the Fourth Eclogue? *Magnus ab integro saeculorum nascitur ordo.* The ordered march of the centuries begins again! Everything tells me, persuades me that we are about to witness the ultimate disorder. Ask Paris! What is being invented there but destruction!

How beautiful it was on the road this morning before dawn. I listened to my own footsteps. And kept one ear open for yours. The only consideration we need is that which we have for each other. The only image of fame we shall have is the one we reflect in each other. Is any territory more vast than mine in your eyes? Or yours in my eyes?

I shall abandon the Father Superior to his college of dry biscuits and black beetles. This time the image is yours. And curiously, re-reading what I have written, I catch myself begging your pardon for these images. They choke my prose-garden like weeds. Pardon? No, I leave that to those moral philosophers who, though they claim to be open-minded, imprison the spirit and stifle their fellow-creatures with each and every precept. The soul is so constituted that nothing can confine it. In the field of action and inspiration it is always out in front of any vanguard. It is the body's scout and needs a body to express itself. What ralliance! Are we inventing words? We have to!

When you receive this letter, I shall already have made a return trip to the Factory of the Sacred Heart of Jesus, to the makers of a Good Conscience. I shall tell them the essential truth: that I can belong only to myself. No soil is more fruitful than one's own. No seasons are more vibrant than those that are welcomed with impatient arms. Every gesture should be relished, every thought embraced.

There. A double knell sounds through this letter intoning its deepest notes. May these intimate words of mine, though some would impotently label them Utopian, herald the start of a successful relationship, the genuine unending modification of one person by another. If there can only be two such people in this world, let us be those two.

Saint-Pardom is a beautiful house. It has a pride that is truly of the South. Pride without grandeur. There are no rooms here that are not redolent of polish and of history. This square two-storeyed building, of sturdy construction, its attics cluttered with old trunks and files, has an indefinable odour that could never belong to the bourgeoisie. Still less to the aristocracy. No, not a trace of either. And what is even better, Saint-Pardom being a halfway house, neither in the town nor the plain, here I feel delightfully midway in everything. It is an ideal place to be oneself and not to have to sacrifice at altars of any kind. Everything here is waxed and varnished. As if my mother had spent her life caressing every nook and cranny of her retreat. In this way she hands her parents' inheritance down to me, intact. And I want so much to add '. . . and so on, from generation to generation'. For we shall each take a wife, you and I. Out of genuine attraction, not in sport. We shall choose women half tough and half tender, midway in everything like us. Closer perhaps to the town than to the plain. We shall give them all those things that women have a right to expect from their husbands. But they will never pierce the secret of our own joint adventure. You see how I pick up fragments of some of your phrases. I have not forgotten a word you wrote to me. Not a single thought. I yield to you.

It took the death of my mother to make me step on to the diving-board of life. Today. Thank you.

And then will come the travelling. We shall have to go round the world first before we realize that we should be tourists in our homeland, for no country is more vast than the one which cast us into the world. I did not shave this morning. I want a moustache, like you! And if you want to bring me a present from Paris, choose a few scores for the piano. In this house the idea of sight-reading music that is different from the music of words cannot help but arouse in me a desire, a kind of longing for pleasure to come. But do not opt for the *Complete Works*(!) of such and such a poet in vogue in the academies or anti-academies of the capital. Poetry is a personal matter. It will remain a tussle between us.

If my calculations are correct, you will arrive thirteen days hence. I shall come and meet you at Cazauban, as you suggested. And I shall have to ask permission of no one but myself. I am my own Father Superior now.

It will be a blazing hot summer, they say. And we shall have a hard task ahead of us. Face to face, we shall have to come to terms with our desire. You after breaking with Paris, I after breaking with the Church. We shall be leaving a whore and a God behind us.

All right, I'm only joking. The idea of your voice haunts me, almost as if I could hear you reading the letter I am writing. But haven't you written the same things to me? I have lost myself in you. You are the fingers of my hand, the look in my eyes, the sound of my footsteps. Yes, how beautiful it was on the road this morning! I was searching for you everywhere. I walked all round the town, and you were there inside me, completely clothed in me.

Towns have teeth. They also have lips. I know you don't trust Paris. And now I am talking, challenging you. Answering you at last!

Tibi,
Joseph.

# First day

How comforting it was for me to copy Joseph's first letter into
this notebook. My handwriting endorsing his. To live all that
again and to live in him again. This is our life. The little rogue in
our flesh. What of the rest? Now it is my turn, Roland's turn, to
write it. It was 7 January 1901. In the diary of our journey I
entered this: 'Taormina. Each time we visit a temple, a site under
excavation, a monument or a church, Joseph is one step ahead of
me. As though he wanted to exclude me from his field of vision.
So then I stop. And he goes on alone, fascinated by all that we had
read and not yet seen. As if all these old stones, standing or lying
around, possessed an astonishing reality that surpassed our
childhood imaginings. Shortly he turns round. Sitting behind a
column or hiding in the shadows of the transept of a church, I
wait for him to call. In that deep hoarse voice. My name. Roland!
And at once this makes one feel cool in the sunshine or hot in the
shade. Joseph is ahead of me. Between us he is constantly creating
a distance that as easily spells violence as affection. An
interrogation!'

This then is what I have enshrined in the tough fibre of words, the
naïve emotion of that day, before it happened: a serious
occurrence, for that is where the diary of this journey ends.
Followed by blank pages, as if scorched by time, crinkled by the
dryness of drawers for so long double-locked until I opened them
again this evening. To let in the daylight! All that remains to mark
the continuity of our life together is this handful of lacerating
fragmentary notes. Even when I have finished telling my story,

11

what was once present will, when the last word has been written, have turned into a past. For we are so anxious, if we fail to make History, to fabricate the past. So keen to leave our mark, although the essence of the union of two human beings can leave no trace behind. Yet today, 12 May 1935, I take it upon myself to relate the events of a day that is past, as though they were present or to come. For they were subsequently to be deeply anchored within each of us, disturbing and tormenting us with a muffled cry for help.

Revolution involves the past. It finds its source in it. Those January days in Taormina the sky hung low, the air was sharp, the sea dark and restless. We had booked into a *pensione* outside the town, in the Viccolo della Palomba, a lane near the old harbour. Soon after we got back from our sightseeing promenades, only partly refreshed by the jars of water we took it in turns to empty over each other's shoulders as we stood with our feet in china basins and then quickly dried ourselves on the rough towels we passed to and fro to warm ourselves up again, we would dress in wool and batiste for the evening, go down to the harbour and on to the jetty to watch the sea at sunset and those fishermen who adventured within a league of the shore to cast their nets out at sea. And there we would wait for the catches, the flash of the fish as they withdrew their lines and their hoop nets, till the moment when night fell around them.

Sandro became our friend. The very first day. As soon as we arrived. As if he had been waiting for us to come off the mailboat. But I need the present tense to tell this story. Not to eternalize it, but out of respect for its throbbing urgency, its ever-enduring vitality. Memories: of those boxes of wriggling insects, coupling and reproducing in that dark night which is the light of day to them. Now it is my turn to flaunt images! Sandro is walking towards us, wild-haired, keen-eyed, with hand outstretched. He catches us unawares, flagrantly stiff and starchy. We are after all only two anonymous travellers rigid with timidity. Yet he chooses *us*. The look in his eyes is one of friendly complicity, suggesting a whole past of shared relationships, a lengthy anticipation finally sanctioned by an embrace. We go along with his little game, or at least with what at first we took to be a kind of sport. We shake him by the hand. He bursts out laughing. And almost jumps for joy. He has a firm handclasp. 'Shake hands,' he says, assuming we are English. Joseph explains to him that we come from the South of France. All this in an Italian that owes more to Latin than to the official language. Sandro looks at Joseph, looks at me. And then, with his two hands he clasps one of ours, each of us in turn. His hands held out flat, with one supporting, the other covering ours, as though to indicate by this unusual gesture of welcome that he will be our guide. Everything is contained in that first gesture.

Sandro leads us to his grandmother's in the Viccolo della Palomba. He says that the rooms she lets are as grand as the local gentry's. He carries our bags. Sniffs the air and advises us to inhale it deeply. Whistles a tune. First we follow him, then we flank him, one on either side. Instinctively I remove my travelling coat. Sandro smiles. Is it on account of that smile that I have never since then buttoned an overcoat, even when the weather is at its coldest? That coat was *de trop*, offered up in tribute. Sicilian winters are mild. Sandro in shirtsleeves with his forearms bare seemed to be taunting me. I felt that I was in fancy dress. And that unlike me he was in communion with the wind, which zigzagged through the narrow alleys, raising the grey dust and ballooning the big white sheets on the rooftops. Joseph too removed his topcoat. We exchanged a look of connivance. Sandro had just wormed his way into our hearts. Perhaps we were going to learn how to travel at last.

Sandro bangs open the shutters of our room. Sandro flings himself full-length on the great bed and bounces his whole body up and down to prove the excellence of the springs. Then, conscious of our embarrassment, he leaps to his feet and straightens everything out, sheet, blanket and pillows. Joseph approaches the window. He is avoiding me. I give Sandro a weak smile. He has understood: only one bed. Putting Joseph and me under an obligation? Or was

13

it a lucky chance to direct and guide us? Sandro pouts and gives a slight shrug of the shoulders. He doubtless thinks we are hypocrites. Again I smile at him. The surprised look on his face disarms me. He is barely sixteen. We are young, too, Joseph and I. All this awkwardness is our means of communication, a silent one in which Sandro participates by opening our cases and carefully putting our clothes away. I remember the creak of the wardrobe door, the precision of Sandro's movements, the look he exchanged with Joseph when he turned round, a look of wounded amusement. And when the cases were empty and the wardrobe was closed and Sandro had gone to fetch the towels and fill up the jugs, Joseph came up to me and whispered: 'This is Hobson's choice. Take it or take it . . .'

In recounting all this, the present tense, being indicative, suits Sandro to perfection, but any system of reference that touches Joseph and myself drives me back into the past. Only natural perhaps when I am trying to prick the meaning out of the life we spent together.

Sandro takes off his shirt and his sandals. With bare chest and bare feet, wearing nothing but his short trousers, he places the jugs and basins on the floor. Lays the towels over a chair and, although there was nothing else we had asked him for, stands and waits, with a glove in one hand and a cube of soap in the other. It is my turn to say to Joseph: 'This is Hobson's choice. Take it or take it!'

Strange rites we submit to, like children. Now it surprises me, when three decades have passed, to speak of strangeness when it was all so spontaneous. It was eleven o'clock in the morning. We had spent an uncomfortable night in a coach crammed with men and women and children and animals of every kind, the whole lot chattering, blubbing, squealing and screeching. We were so squashed up against each other that when the light came we even found it hard to catch a glimpse through the carriage door of the slopes of Etna or make out the sea or the horizon. Sandro had just given bodily movement back to us. And in celebration he was inviting us to baptism by water.

It was then, having spread my clothes out on the bed and with a buzzing in my head that prevented me taking a light-hearted view of the situation, that I had the impression I was seeing myself and seeing Joseph naked for the very first time. Yet at college, spring, winter or autumn, how many times had we showered side by side, splashing each other, dripping that wishy-washy water that Joseph called Jesuitical, because it was too holy? But here, forming a triangle, Sandro is watching us. I discover Joseph's body just as, staring straight at me in some amazement, he discovers my body, from top to toe, fully grown. Mature? As though sprung out of some strange cocoon, adults of twenty-odd years, we could at last eye each other and take the measure of the immeasurable growth of our bodies, lovingly sculpted from the surface of our skin to the supplest of our muscles by those years of marching and wrestling, rambling and truancy. A perfect picture both of us, which we each discovered at the same time as Sandro, who was amused by the embarrassment we were scarcely able to conceal.

The water we let him pour over us, each standing in his own basin, had a special quality. An unaccustomed freshness. It was water that we shared.

Sandro puts the first jug down, soaps Joseph's back and then his front, moving Joseph's hands aside to reveal his private parts. My eyes take in the clearly defined curve of Joseph's hips, his shoulders, his wrists and the nape of his neck. So all this is Joseph? This 'all' catches me by surprise. Then Sandro turns to me. He indicates to Joseph that he must rub himself to work up the foam. Sandro soaps my back and then my front. I move my hands aside and reveal my private parts. Sandro smiles at me and rubs me vigorously. He takes a step back and indicates that I too should work up some foam. Then Sandro lifts up the arms of each of us in turn and rubs the soap under our armpits. He starts whistling again and then questions us with a '*Piacere?*'

Then he picks up the second jug and with a constant little stream of water rinses us down, taking care not to splash too much over the floor. Finally he wraps the towels round our shoulders and dries us briskly, first one then the other. Two other towels to finish the ritual as he kneels by the basin to dry our feet. Joseph blushed. So did I. Sandro pours the dirty water into a large ewer. '*Scusi.*' He leaves the room. Joseph throws his wet towel over a chair. I do the same. Joseph clenches his fists and at some distance from me takes up a boxing position in jest. I do the same in self-defence. We laugh. Fear of commitment?

Sandro is wiping the floor and cleaning out the basins. He goes in and out, bringing the jugs back full of water and putting them on the washstand with some clean towels. Neither Joseph nor I have dressed again. Everything is clean and tidy as it was before. With his arms folded Sandro takes a long look at us. He drops his eyes and crosses his feet to rub his toes. Then he turns, walks to the door and bolts it from the inside. He makes for the window and closes the shutters. '*Prego . . .*' He smiles at us. Moves to the bed, takes his trousers off and, naked, lies full length on it, right in the middle with his head between the two pillows, hands folded behind his neck. '*Siamo amici, vero?*'

Joseph and I exchanged glances. Which of us would be the first to say 'Hobson's choice' again? But nothing in this account of the events that occurred on 5, 6 and 7 January in the first year of this century should be taken as titillation. What happened to us that first day and the days that followed was the culmination of our urgent need for an exchange, for the clash of flesh, of those immense sexual organs, our bodies.

Spellbound, conscious of our distance from each other and from the bed, we eyed one another, listening to the sounds from outside, the beating of the wind, people passing in the Viccolo, the twelve chimes of midday repeated as if in echo from the bell-towers of several churches, and then a muffled footstep in the corridor of the *pensione*. The grandmother? Sandro beckons us. I am the first to move. Joseph joins us. All three stretched out trembling on the bed, roughly, we collided.

And that was the moment when our journey really began. All our journeys and adventures. All the rest! A new life, obliterating the old. Sandro had the brown salty skin of the sea. I can recall him now: with his eyes wide open he kisses Joseph first. Forces Joseph to open his eyes. Then with his hand on my back he forces my face down to his chest. I can hear the beat of his heart. A beating heart. Strong and muted. As if the whole earth had started knocking at this one point. And on Sandro's lips I discovered the imprint of Joseph's lips. That was our first kiss.

In discovering our bodies we had inadvertently stumbled on something else as well: the unexpectedness of complete fulfilment, the total unreality of all established appearances. The pleasure came to us, all three of us, without need to touch each other. And in this our first embrace neither my lips nor my hands nor my body even brushed against Joseph. Between us, arching his back from side to side, Sandro offered himself to each of us, keeping us apart in order, who knows, to bring us closer together? And always there will lie between us the body of Sandro Prego, Mister Shake-Hands, Siamo Amici, all the names we shall invent in tragic memory of our young companion.

And if I announce it as tragic, it is because of what happened after the writing of these last travel notes. You might say in the blank pages.

Sandro wipes us down. He laughs, kisses me on the belly, ties the soiled towel round his hips and walks to the window, where he bangs the shutters open, beats his fists against the guardrail and shouts. A raucous yell as if to notify the wind and the sky. With his eyes shut and his head back. Later, over lunch at the harbour, Sandro runs through the list of everything he wants to show us in the days to come. How long are we staying, he asks. We answer 'a few days . . .' with no precision. And with a shrug of the shoulders he murmurs 'Sempre'. Sandro Sempre!

17

For two whole days and nights we followed him everywhere. The word *stranieri* seemed to open every door to us. Sandro knows everything about everything. 'Who told you that?' No answer, but he crosses the fingers of both hands, the middle finger over the index, as if to ward off a spell. And the first evening, like the second, he says '*prego*' when just about to leave us and follows us into the room. He gets the bed ready, draws the bolt and closes the shutters. Kneeling in the middle of the bed, facing us and between us, a staggered threesome, he gazes at us, grasps us with both hands and then lies flat on his stomach, his face buried in the sheet, mumbling '*Tutto*'. Repeating '*Tutto*'. Everything?

The third day as on every other day at the close of the afternoon we go and watch Sandro from the end of the dyke. He has promised to catch a marvellous fish for us, for the three of us, for dinner. Standing in the stern of his boat he waves his arms to us as he leaves the harbour. There is a low sky. And a hot wind from the south. An unpredictable fickle wind. Curling the foam or whipping deep. Joseph remarks that Sandro is the only one to leave the harbour. Not one boat on the horizon. Sandro, sole master of his craft, takes in a sail, fixes the helm, belays the sheet and shouts both our names, which reach us in bursts. He bends over, seizes the nets with both hands and casts them overboard. Suddenly the wind switches. The boat turns over. Joseph springs to his feet: 'Sandro!' I leap up too. I grip Joseph's arm. He pulls away. All there is is the hull of the boat tossed by the waves. Nothing else, nothing, not a face, not a hand. Did it cross my mind for a moment that Sandro was staying under water to give us a fright? I started running from rock to rock to get closer to the sea. A swirling wind. A precipitation of sky and clouds. How many times, impotently, have we called our friend's name? How many? 'But what are they waiting for . . .?'

At last two other boats come to the rescue, harpoon the hull and tow it in. Sandro has not reappeared. We return to the harbour. Joseph keeps saying. 'He's there underneath, still breathing . . . trapped like a prisoner, that's all.' But when, panting, we reach the quayside, men are diving, disappearing and reappearing, making signals of disaster to the other fishermen. Harpoons, ropes and the hull is righted. There in the water-filled craft lies the body of Sandro, caught in the nets with bleeding fists. A woman next to us explains that he did not die at once, that he has been beating against the shell of the boat. She quotes the names of other fishermen. More women run up, crossing themselves. The men lift Sandro's body and lay it down on the quay. Respectfully we move aside. And when I feel impelled to go nearer, Joseph restrains me. Maintaining a strong grip on me for quite a long time. Till I was trembling. And when he released me, it was my turn to hold on to him. And there we remained, at a distance, until Sandro's body was borne away. Night falls early, in January.

Yes, night has fallen heavily, all at once, this evening, 12 May 1935, thirty-four years later. When my wife Sabine came to Saint-Pardom, her sister Clothilde pretended she had forgotten all the quarrels that had divided them for so many years. In front of her sister, Clothilde asked me to close Joseph's eyes for the last time. And Sabine smiled. She is the one who has never been afraid of death. And she perhaps is the one who has never given meaning to her life. I went to the bed. I slid my hand over Joseph's forehead and very slowly I stroked his eyelids down. And as my hand slipped away, it brushed against his lips. Farewell.

I am not just writing, Joseph, I am writing you. One always writes someone else. I am not just recreating or recreating Joseph. Back here again at Copeyne, handing you over to our wives, loving rival sisters whom we learnt to love, I want to surround you with an accompanying silence and raise you up on high, while everything in me is still vibrating with the fluidity of life. Us! Our joint creation! And so this evening I have reread the letter in which you called out to me. And so, even before I summon your son, your first-born, and your daughter, together with my first-born, my daughter, and my son, our four children, to join us at once to take you to your last resting-place, that 'inside-out home' as you used to call it, so too I want with these words not so much to hand on our creation as to bear witness to it. We shall open the TERREFORT vault. Will your mother's coffin still be as white as it was that day you wrote your first letter?

Only a few hours ago I was reading to you at your bedside. Livy, the pages where you left your bookmark. Could you hear me? Writing is the only true outrage, a notebook, this notebook, a labyrinth of narratives, which like the skin of our bodies can alone release the soul, the essence of everything. An ongoing spirit. Like a forward wind. A guiding spirit.

Joseph has only just died: on 12 May 1935. But time is not governed by dates. All that counts now, to summon up your presence, hand of my hand, heart of my heart, is what came to pass in the time between. The time between is all. So when shall we admit the harmony and the stabbing truth of our lives? When shall we accept our desires? Tears are a weapon of the soul. My wife Sabine is helping Clothilde. Clothilde is joining her husband Joseph's hands. Family tableau! Clothilde is folding a rosary round your hands, Joseph. As though to bind them. Now you are back in the fold! Some good Father may even come in final irony to bless your remains. Then the trick will have been played. But I shall write. I shall tell. And the clamour will reawaken us. For not a day has passed without my realizing that our most blatant, most unifying feature lay in all the uncertainties of our language. I know that this evening you are restraining me. As you did in the harbour of Taormina. You are restraining me. And you are still trembling. I am still in the grip of that embrace as I go on writing in the attempt to lay bare, beneath the caparison of events and incidents in our lives, the quivering flanks of life.

Our memories are still to come! And if I hum as I recount them, it is because everything must be done, as Sandro did it, with an accompanying whistle. It is music from the soul, embracing the wind. Music no sooner sounded than wafted away.

There. I have my own remembrance and your letters, a few pieces that you wrote and those I am about to write, I shall consecrate my nights to them, *our* nights still. For some time past, as you know, Sabine sleeps in a separate bedroom and no longer speaks to me. Your death is her victory.

I can see you on our way home from Taormina. We are stopping for the night at Matelica. During the day we had visited the sanctuary of Loreto on the Adriatic and lingered a long time in front of Leopardi's house. You seemed to be happy. But at Matelica you suddenly get up in the middle of the night and standing on the bed you start beating your fists against the wall, calling for Sandro. Yes, Joseph, the earth itself has turned turtle and holds us prisoners, you, me and him, now and for ever. And you are hammering on the wall and I have thrown my arms around you. You see, you are still alive! You live! I shall tell them all, you hear me? I shall write everything down.

# Second day

It is not my intention here to prove anything. Just barely suggest a tentative approach. Joseph has just died. All I can do through these notes is bring him back to me and thus attribute to myself a brief moment of survival after death.

In order to do this, I shall employ all the materials at my disposal. From my memory, as little as possible. That way the text will stand at one remove, like a sketch for a novel. I distrust my memory, for now it is a memory halved. In Joseph I had found my twin again, born from fluid from the same sac. Our real parents were in fact my father, guilty of tolling a bell, and his mother, condemned for a guilty passion. How could I truly examine our past life when now I am alone and can retain only half of it? Joseph's death has made me a receiver of stolen goods.

Above all I shall utilize those writings of Joseph's which are in my possession and those from my own pen which he gave to me a few days ago when for the first time he realized he was doomed. But again I must make clear that he did not entrust these documents to me in order that I should use them. Neither was it on the understanding that I should destroy them. He passed them on to me, that's all. Perhaps with the vague idea that they might help me.

And finally I shall use, but without alteration, my own notes and writings. And once again, the dates will be there only as a lure into the present, though they help to create a logical development.

Thus it is by three methods that I shall try to prolong our lives for a short time more into the time to come. It will be an adventure, perhaps the only real one, one that is shared and truly human, the adventure of friendship or love. And we liked neither of those words. We were only too willing to substitute poetry or companionship. For there lies the bond and the binding. The relationship we had with Nature was the principal source of our own. There can surely be no accord between two beings that does not spring from the mutual contemplation of the same scene in Nature. What one shares first of all is the vast body of the world. Then there is no valley, no stream that fails to remind one of one's partner and the geography of that other body. There is no wind, however cruel or inviting, that fails to conjure up a look from that friend, one's own beloved poet. How can one speak of poetry in an age that assesses everything in terms of quantity and qualification, in which invention, categorization and speed govern all, at the start of a century that hammers out in forecast the end of an era, eager, impatient, as we know it is, to dissipate all values of mind and spirit and sacrifice all sense of individuality; how can one speak of a poetry like ours at such a time?

And if we (what joy it is, Joseph, to say we!) hand on not a single one of our poems, it is not only because we destroyed them as soon as they were written and we had shown them to one another, but also and chiefly because poetry does not reside in poems. Poetry is all around us, it lies between, beneath and within us, it is everywhere but in those tombstone-words. The perfect excuse for two poets who failed in their task? No, ever since that day when as children we first swapped our pencil-cases, we always wanted it that way. Unwittingly we had just interchanged our instruments of torture. Unwittingly we had just completed an act of union. Pencils, pen-holders and rubbers in their funereal black-lacquered cases were a perfect image of the surface-element in writing: window-dressing! And this extravagant gesture that first united us uplifted us both. Every poem that Joseph Terrefort wrote for Roland Raillac could be nothing but a pale shadow of the transparent reality of our natural selves in which Nature was inherent. Every poem that Roland Raillac wrote for Joseph Terrefort could be nothing but the reflection of a reflection, an illusion on paper. Poetry can be recognized, but not written down. What is written down circumscribes it. It cannot be inscribed. It may be stroked and caressed, but never fully embraced. The embrace is never absolute. Never perfect. Always there is something missing, even in the simplest cases, the cry of a bird, the rustle of a leaf, a shifting change of light, or in the most complex examples those points of contact with living things and creatures so subtle in range and intensity that they slip from the grasp of form. As poets Joseph and I used to think of ourselves as manipulators of content. Against the false aesthetics which sometimes, for a brief spell only, provoked our admiration, we would oppose a stubborn determination to produce and discard, to attempt and reject, to draw on our innermost secrets, our bodies' most intimate depths, intermingling. With us everything implodes. It still does.

Our most beautiful poems were born of our gestures and our glances. For poetry there was, between us and within us, impelling each of us towards the other. In all our thoughts and actions we jostled one another. We clashed and battled with sensations. Our tranquillity was filled with fury. Our fury was serene. Not a day was spent, one without the other. I arrive at Cazauban. I return from Paris with my diploma and my honorary title of Postal Inspector (at twenty-two, what a Republic!), and from this moment we shall never leave each other. Even yesterday, Joseph, you did not leave me. You will not leave me till the very last line of this unfinished, unfinishable, text.

In my luggage at Cazauban there was no volume of *Complete Works* by this or that famous poet. No. For years and years, each time you show me or I show you a poem, each time it will be the turn of one of us to laugh and say: 'Here's another for our *Incomplete Works!*' And we will tear these fixed set pieces of writing into shreds to search in our embrace for that totality of words and signs that we were never able to set down on paper.

In my luggage at Cazauban there were a few scores, the sonatas of Mozart. A revelation for you and for me. And we shall never tire of this music. It is one step ahead of us. Talk about it and it seems perpetually asking to be deciphered. On the cover of this collection you wrote in capital letters: 'The interpretation of the following pages demands a total surrender of the person to the work.' That is what you wrote on it the summer of our reunion, and a similar spirit applies to what I am attempting now. And I never heard you interpret any of those sonatas twice in the same manner. Of course you were affected by the weather, the seasons, the happenings of the day, the ordinary little things on the surface of life. There was also the deeper current of our quest. You did not play those sonatas for me or for yourself, but for us, somewhere just ahead of us, secretly hoping that you could capture the music at its source.

In my luggage at Cazauban there was nothing from Paris. Not one memory. Not one object. Not even one item of their fashionable clothes. What I brought with me in fact was the lightest baggage of all: a whole period of time to come. How this notebook inspires me!

I shall evade nothing and spare no one, for our encounters have taught us never to spare ourselves. Our poetry found its own burrow, it can dig in and curl up anywhere. And if now at times the sordid and the acceptable rub shoulders, that is because, whatever the censors may say, the two are inextricable, have always been and ever shall be. Accept our love? As we accepted our poetry, our incomplete works, all those torn-up poems! Two incomplete works to make up one dual creation.

I am watching 'us'. I am stepping off the train that day at Cazauban. Joseph is waiting for me. He sees me but does not approach. I put my suitcases down and observe him from a distance. He is not smiling. He plunges into me. He penetrates deep inside, everywhere, as if making a thorough examination, to seek out any alien symptoms and make sure I am whole and intact. And I plunge into him to find warmth and happiness of every kind again. Inside him I brush ferns and bushes aside. I cross over rivers. I breathe in the dust from our pathways. I listen to the silence of our hours of study at college in the evenings before dormitory-time. I rediscover unquiet moments of every kind, meetings and evasions, and in him too I find everything whole and intact. And only then, advancing at the same second, did we move towards one another. A clasping of hands. Then all at once Joseph pinches my cheek and says: 'Where on earth were you? I've been looking everywhere.' And it is my turn to pinch his: 'Just behind you.' And we laugh.

Cares and chagrins, do your worst! What we created eludes your categories! You talk of politics, but what can you mean by politics in this century, when it nibbles at everything and gnaws away at our world? There is only one political act that counts, the action that creates a couple and organizes their lives. Yes, Joseph's skin was political all right. Contact with it varied every time and its capacity for alteration had the power to alter me. We used it to forge a place for ourselves in the city of our dreams. What a feat of organization! The uniting of two human beings just as Nature unites her seasons.

At Cazauban Joseph insists on carrying my bags: 'How light they are!' In reply I say something like: 'I've only brought back what I took away with me.' He smiles. These are our *Joint Works*. And when the last line is written I shall only have to say it again: 'These are our *Joint Works*!'

How dear is this desk round which we find ourselves for our final combat. You and me, Joseph!

Sabine has just come home. She is waiting to have dinner with me. I love Sabine for being harsh and distant, for the contempt she bears me, for the joy she conceals today, for the wild love she has for Henri, my eldest son, your godson, because he could become what in her view I have never been. Sabine is the town. The family showcase. One must be successful, mustn't one?

Sabine is waiting for me downstairs. Believing that we are separated for ever, she does not realize that we are still together.

Tomorrow our children will be arriving from Bordeaux, Toulouse and Paris. A family reunion, centred upon you, down there in the village of the dead, so close to the town of the living. Yet you will be in here, waiting for me, impatient for these notes to be resumed. I can already hear you, forbidding me to trim, elaborate or disguise. If we are to find a true expression of ourselves, out of these fragments should emerge and take shape the eventual outline of a pair of human beings, the poetic couple. And each fragment shall remain as it has always been: anticipatory. And every admission shall reflect an image of all the ambushes we laid for one another!

I open this notebook as I once opened your pencil-case, the one you gave me. I shall forget my own self totally and subordinate everything to the expression of what we created together. What a sonata, we two!

I shall return quickly from the cemetery. And I shall copy *our* portrait into this notebook. First the one you made of me. Then the one I sketched of you. Portraits we exchanged on our return from Taormina. We did not throw them away because we did not think of them as poems, but as relics! Who knows? They bore all the marks of gravity we had just discovered about each other: through our bodies. And about our bodies I shall tell everything. At least I shall go as far as we were able to go. Vast terrains over which we shall never travel extensively enough. Sabine is calling me.

# 25 August 1901. My portrait, by Joseph

Each vision of you, Roland, is a point of no return. This first line touches on caricature. It springs from me, rather than from you. It is the emanation of an impression that is constantly renewed. Every time I see you, you are different, inviting a different judgement. Am I giving too much away at the start? As though, in order to draw your portrait, I wanted to say everything at once to force myself to find something more to say.

Every transformation in you, every time, every day, has the power to modify me. If I use the term 'no return' to describe your volatile nature, that bodily presence which the slightest glance from you imposes and intensifies, it is because the sight of you proves to me that I am not alone, that every thought of mine, wherever I am, is not single but dual; this sentiment enfolds me and invites me to take the lead, without ever having to look back. That is why at times I am ahead of you.

I promised a portrait of you. You are composing mine at the very same time in a neighbouring room. What in theory is no more than a stylistic exercise between friends, a sort of holiday task for late afternoons in August, almost a game, is also a challenge when our two images blend so well together. So I shall really have to separate you from me, create a distance between us as an artist would and simply ask myself: 'What is there that is different about him, specifically him?' I need to borrow the jargon of the police! 'Distinctive features of Raillac, Roland, please?'

Your eyes are neither green nor blue. Green when you gaze at the woods and meadows. Blue when you tilt your head up to contemplate the sky. Blue too when you cross the waters of the Verse to join me on the opposite bank, for as you told me: 'I am swimming in the reflection of the sky.' Beautiful all that. It comes out magnified. I know how easy it is to sound suspect, when one tries to write down one's impression of another.

Yes, Constable, his body is my point of no return and all Nature is reflected in his eyes!

Raillac, Roland, is shorter than I am. My kiss almost lands on the tip of his nose. But don't make a note of that, Constable, it offends current standards of morality. A peck on the tip of a nose is not exactly virile, is it? And yet where height is concerned, it's the first thing to notice.

His skin is soft and smooth, one slips and slides over it. He is hard. Made of rock. Even when he's drowsy, all of him is firm and taut, and there I go talking about him as though he were some beast. Yes, in a way Roland is a beast, a crazy little animal that grew up like me, fed on the same grain, in the same fields where we were thrown together, trying to roll the earth round our bodies like a vast blanket. Beating our fists against the hull of the sky.

His eyebrows grow together till they meet. His hair is chestnut, which is another way of saying fair in the summer under the sun's caress and brown in winter under a muffled sky. Roland is a passing cloud. Never the same. He drifts where he will. He knows where he's going. And he takes me with him. Talking of him I fall back on all those images we both dislike. Really, Roland, this isn't a very serious game! But as I'm still waiting for you to bring me my portrait, I must go on circling round you, to pin you down.

Your hands are long, broad and massive. Enveloping hands which could almost lift you up in their palms and protect you like a fallen bird. Clasping, brandishing hands, hands so immense they

29

confer immensity on everything. The hands of a bell-ringer who all by himself can toll the knell in the Cathedral of Saint-Pierre and so jangle the bells that they alert the whole population of a goodly township. Hands which for centuries have furrowed out the fields of Copeyne. Hands made for rolling out barrels of Armagnac. Hands for throwing nets, as big as a district, to ensnare wood-pigeons. Hands to rock the tables in the Café du Commerce when someone is seeking to impress, or in the Café du Lion d'Or when the talk turns to politics. Hands that bear the weight of history, like the lowest branches of a genealogical tree. Heavy hands that make a hollow when laid on my belly. 'You asleep again? Wake up . . .' Hands like a voice, rough and deep, that gives to every syllable of every word a burst of sound and an echo. The echo of messages heard and perpetuated over centuries spent working the same land and rejoicing in the same terrain.

The true portrait of my friend Roland can be summed up in his name: RAILLAC. A face, a grin. Life.

You have marks on your shoulders like the map of a world of unknown continents, lands of fire and icecaps. Not freckles but brown patches, like beauty spots that have spread. You often ask me with a laugh to teach you the geography of the world you carry round on your shoulders, so I make up names of places, seas and islands; and when, tired of invention, I descend the great valley of your back, I discover a whole ocean, calm and featureless, upon which I can sail. How many have emigrated from your town, gone down the Garonne and pulled themselves up by the roots in search of the Americas? This is *my* greatest voyage, and my undiscovered countries can all be epitomized on your shoulders. I lean over you to look. And you ask me: 'What can you see today?'

Your moustache is uncouth, bushy and drooping. Whereas mine is delicate, pointed and upturning, a shade too elegant. I look after mine, whereas you allow yours to grow wild. Each time you are about to speak you moisten your lips. You announce your words with the tip of your tongue, suggestive of *gourmandise*. One word and your mouth is watering. And that makes my mouth water too. I am unable to draw your portrait without including mine. Your footsteps are heavy, almost resonant. A steady, almost insistent tread. I often asked you why you made so much noise when you climbed the stairs at Saint-Pardom. And you always answered: 'I don't like losing touch with the earth. I'm uneasy with stairs and storeys. I make use of them, but they are foreign to my nature.' For long I took that to be a kind of joke. But joking is not our style. So once my attention was drawn to it, I couldn't help noticing that when we're having a meal in a wayside inn you very often take your shoes off under the table. Or remembering all those sandals you used to lose in our childhood summers, when you'd kick them off at the start of our hike and leave them at the edge of the forest or hidden under some stone. 'I like to feel the crunch of the earth, cracking beneath my feet!' And when the excursion was over and we'd made our way back to our starting point – if ever we could find it again – those sandals would have gone astray.

You very often ask me questions that contain the answer. Only your eyes convey true interrogation.

So you often leave me the responsibility of making choices of every kind. Where shall we go? Wherever you like! What do you want to drink? Whatever you want! Or even worse: the same as you! The only wishes that you impose and that really spring from your choosing are those you refrain from putting into words. Yet you told me just to write and write and on no account monitor the sketching of this portrait. But you are taking your time with your thumbnail sketch of me. Now I'm getting impatient. What have you discovered about me?

I jump a page and sum up: your eyebrows grow together till they meet, your shoulders contain continents, your hands are enormous, your eyes are the colour of the surrounding scenery and your feet take root in the earth. What have I missed out? Your navel? It is curiously deep. As if your mother too had wanted to hang on to you. As if she had done her utmost to put off your appearance till the very last moment. You, the son of an old man who returned from Cayenne in the early days of the Third Republic. For your father's homecoming there was such a pealing of the bells, they still talk about it now.

Your sex is dark brown, almost black. There is Arab blood in our veins. The blood of invaders. Centuries pass and the finger of Allah emerges all-conquering from the lower part of your belly.

Just now you said to me: 'Write, write, don't stop, dip your pen without looking at the inkwell. Don't pause for paragraphs any more than you can help. I want my portrait to be a portfolio of sketches. You'll see what mine is like. I'll be able to outline you with one stroke.' All your most commonplace remarks begin with, 'Look . . .' You are a child, Roland, in the body of a boxer. Roland, champion of the steadyweight class! 'Look . . .' you say, as if you were afraid I'm not seeing what you have seen. Is it really possible to share everything?

When you are seated, you never cross your legs. You keep them slightly apart, you lay your hands flat on your knees and straight as a steeple you look at people you don't like at a point just over their heads and beyond them. 'Raillac, lower your eyes when I'm talking to you!' How many times did the Father Superior punish you for that haughty, skimming look of yours? 'He's bald,' you'd explain with a laugh, 'and I skate right over to the other side!'

You have a sense of humour. When you're amusing that means you're bored. You love words that skid off into different meanings, literal nonsense, simple spoonerisms and the flattest statements of the obvious. There's something over-anxious about your humour. You laugh even before you can verify whether what you've just said has provoked laughter or not. And the others are amused just to see that you're amused. You shine in company that you detest for people who make a fuss of you: 'We must invite him, he's so amusing.' Or, 'He's so terribly wicked.' Then you say to me: 'Come on, we'll leave. I feel ashamed.' You are ashamed of the show you put on. You wonder at everything, so you're a wonder at playing the fool.

At night you sleep like a rock. You lie down, go straight off to sleep and never move again. In the morning no sooner have you opened your eyes than you've sprung out of bed. As though you'd had a fright or been taken by surprise. You blunder about a bit, bump into the doors and the walls. Sometimes you pretend that you grumble in fun, but in fact you're furious that day has dawned. You go for water to splatter all over your face with the open palms of your hands, as if you wanted to slap yourself. Your ablutions are a battle to wake yourself up. I've never been able to think of it in any other way. Really you regret the immobility that you have just surrendered, the mysterious dominion of sleep. This above all is not the time to speak to you. One must wait until you are wiping your mouth after coffee, or stretching yourself after breakfast. Or not even then but later. Your first word will concern the nature of the weather. And this is not just an Anglo-Saxon politeness, but a greeting pure and simple. 'Warm, . . .' you say, or, 'Raining . . .' You announce the day.

This portrait of mine is trying to catch a resemblance, though dissimilarities define a likeness best. No harmony is sweeter than the disharmonies in that Mozart sonata which you love so much and which I play without your asking when you have been silent for too long.

You are a creature perpetually in ambush. A fearful beast skulking behind me, in order presumably to make it all the easier to spring. You seek your prey everywhere, for everywhere there is truth, and there is nothing you love more than tearing off masks wherever you find them.

Raillac Roland is irredeemable. And so he will remain till the end, desperate as he is to claim and proclaim his right to exist. In this world. In this century. In me.

33

There is nothing that brings us closer than the coincidence of pleasure when our inflamed bodies can embrace no more. And when you find release, you open your eyes wide and gaze at me. And that wild look is your portrait. Only then are you no longer master of yourself. For me our game is over now. Is it any good going on, Roland?

# 25 August 1901. Joseph's portrait, by me. In exchange

Joseph Terrefort lives as he breathes. That is his unique characteristic, and I shall make use of it in tracing this portrait of him. The idea for this exchange came to me last night. He thinks I'm sleeping when in fact I'm watching him. As we agreed to exchange these pages in token of our friendship, this revelation runs a strong risk of modifying our relationship yet again. Now he will know that I keep my eye on him.

I shall scribble down in my small cramped handwriting, my catspaw scrawl so different from his which is large and pleasing, the impressions I get when I listen to him breathing.

Joseph Terrefort has a long, delicate, aquiline nose. When he is breathing naturally, at the piano for example, his cheeks are slightly hollowed, his chin drawn in and his nostrils flare imperceptibly. He is quite unconscious of it. It is almost comical.

I have watched his nose get bigger and his face take shape. It's marvellous to think how everything grows, in one's head too, develops into ridges or folds. Yes, Joseph Terrefort's head is getting knobblier with time. The process goes on indefatigably. Everything starts with the muscles in the nostrils which pull in here, hollow out there. Little by little, unknowingly and no doubt involuntarily, Joseph Terrefort is sculpting the face of his father, Dr Rigand the brigand! And if I have just used a nickname that Joseph dislikes, it is not to give vent to the kind of humour he so often reproaches me with, and which does in fact at times redound on me, but in order to draw the broad outline which will lend the right proportions and with luck some fidelity to the picture I want to trace in these lines and then present to him.

It is however the writer's wish that this should be seen as a portrait *in words*, as no draughtsman's technique can reconstitute the fluidity of a breathing, living image.

Very often, when I am sharing the same room with Joseph Terrefort for several hours at a stretch, there are times when I feel I am stifling, so I get up and open a window. The cause is not suffocation or some disturbance of the psyche or any physical malfunction of my respiratory tracts. No, the whole truth is that Joseph Terrefort absorbs great volumes of air, and the air he selects is the purest. His nostrils make a positive choice, they detect the very best of the air in circulation and literally snatch it away from anyone else. Nothing is pure enough for Joseph Terrefort and in this respect this noble personage deserves to be treated with consideration.

No irony should be read into this. This is a serious portrait. If we look back to the childhood of our model, it is worth noting how allergic he was to the perfumes worn by his wicked mother on those occasions when she visited the college. 'When shall I see her as she really is?' he would ask, gripping me by the arm when later he returned from the visitors' parlour. He never dared mention the heady perfume by name, but the expression on his face and in the centre of it a twitch of his nose would give it all away. It would be several hours before he stopped pulling faces.

When at Mass he happened to be officiating next to me, he would always put me in charge of the censer. Or if ever it amused me to insist on him performing this duty, he would hold it away from him at arm's length, as though it were a repulsive object diffusing spiralling odours that 'made him feel quite sick'.

In both cases, in order to revive himself, he would start taking his breath in gulps. Then I would poke fun at him and call him 'Puffing Billy' or 'Ravenous Rabbit'. Such images speak for themselves. But don't let their colourfulness mislead you into underestimating their gravity.

Whatever happened to Joseph Terrefort's little-boy nose? A tremulous nose, well able in the refectory to express by a discreet quiver its amused disgust with some specific dish. Or the nose that refrained from inhaling if we went anywhere near the kitchens. In fact it was a very serious matter, the revitalization of his whole body. Let us say that Joseph Terrefort has never liked outlandish smells. Or, even worse, common and familiar ones.

At recreation time he was always the first to race to the farthest corner of the playground, where he would jump up on the little wall, cling on to a terracotta urn, always the same one, the furthest removed from the others and from everyone else, and then say: 'I feel like Ulysses out at sea, sniffing the sea breezes.' Draw the nose and you'll find out everything about him! A little turned-up nose which the passage of time and the ageing of its owner has made more pointed, like someone sticking out an arm to indicate the way. One really has to be the friend of such a creature not to find a nose like that pretentious, when it robs you of the finest air around, is constantly pointing out the direction his eyes are following and passing judgement of every kind on everything.

Joseph Terrefort sleeps on his back, with his head arched and his hands folded over his chest, like an effigy. The desire for sleep is a torture to him and he is not rewarded with much. In the struggle to obtain some, in his stubborn pursuit of rest he lies in that terribly still horizontal position and imposes upon himself a rhythmical pattern of breathing that gets slower and slower, more and more measured and deliberate till it becomes almost mechanical. So that for anyone near him, listening, sharing his bed or in the one next to his, this can arouse something approaching panic. Is he, like some who would bury their face in a pillow, trying to stifle himself? Does he want to put an end to it all?

Lying next to him, I can see his nose in profile, the highest point against the light or the night, for he always sleeps on the window side. Through that nose everything is breathed in and breathed out. And it is then that Joseph Terrefort gives me the impression he is inhaling less and less and exhaling more and more. He has no love for himself. He is wishing for death.

The above conclusion may appear hasty, dangerous, elliptical, but somewhere inside me one certainty is growing: by day and by night, and with a particular preference perhaps for the night, Joseph Terrefort is constantly, and with every day that passes, apprenticing himself to death.

Sometimes when he looks at me I can sense his eyes brushing over me. Then I can hear and feel his breath more acutely. Always cool or cold. Strange, a human being who fabricates coldness.

This is not a satirical portrait either. The person it is destined for will know how to discard superficialities and fleeting impressions when what I am trying to do is to trace in words the course of those winds that sweep through the depths of his being, the dark recesses of his body, sucked in only to be expelled again. The grotto within is barred to me. All I can do is examine those which explore and seek to penetrate the walls of his spongy fibrous world of tissues, threaded with subterranean brooks and rivulets that deliver their finest treasure to their despoiler: their life-giving oxygen! And if at times – with my eyes almost closed, used as I am never to reveal by the merest quiver that I am still awake – I fall into a doze, then I break into the same calm and restful breathing pattern as my neighbour.

Sometimes too, for reasons Joseph Terrefort does not wish to give and I no longer wish to enquire into, at the end of one of our walks when we have put two or three leagues behind us and tackled several woods, cut a diagonal path through the meadows and followed the gentle ridges of a rosary of hills, he suddenly complains of feeling out of breath and turning to face me, being then ahead of me, asks me to slow the pace!

This paradoxical behaviour is paralleled in another way: when he is happy, pleased with a landscape or a meal, touched by some confidential exchange of views or, feeling at odds with all those who seek our company, relieved to find himself once again alone with me – then he expels a series of deep-drawn sighs, as if in exasperation! Since our return from Taormina, I have stopped breathing: Joseph Terrefort breathes for me. By the grace of Sandro I have crossed the gulf that used to yawn between our beds as children, and now, curled up against him, his rhythm has become mine. And I should add that this curious phenomenon is as much due to him as to me, as much to his impulsion towards me as to the curiosity that drives me to know him better and to plumb his depths.

Yes, I am jealous of what lies within him. Closer examination has its dangers. Something tells me that Joseph Terrefort harbours pain he does not wish to complain of, a sorrow he wishes to silence, some secret sickness that only thrives on asphyxia, so that in struggling against it he imposes upon himself a respiratory rhythm that purifies him by breathing deeply and with great deliberation.

So there he is, lifting his head, gazing at the horizons of our domain, all the earth, the whole world confined within the boundaries of our town, so completely do we contain it. There he is, breathing in these salubrious breezes. The winds that bring salvation are converging on him.

This is not a lyrical statement. It etches into sharp relief. A concave feature, like a furrow. This is not a whimsical, a self-indulgent portrait. Let Joseph Terrefort recognize himself by, and for, all those elements in him which in turn inhale and exhale, inspire and expire, inspiring me.

And if I go to open a window in order to breathe, because I have been sharing the air for too long in a room where we were sacrificing to those gentle or brutal ritual exchanges, without which we could never survive our day-to-day existence, it is not and never will be an ironical gesture of reprisal. Robust as he is, Joseph Terrefort is none the less suffering from some *malaise* in the most secret part of himself. Either astonished or irritated by it, he prefers to confront it in silence and never speaks of it. Who is there to treat him but his father, the one and only doctor in this town?

At night I have a long time to wait for Joseph Terrefort's breathing to settle; for that little whistle to be silenced, unnoticeable by day but seeming to me in the waiting stillness of the night to be more like a sharp stabbing cry, a sound that rasps and scrapes and pierces like a gimlet, a tireless sound as though his illness had to be constantly drowned by it to stop him losing the battle going on inside.

There is a frailty here in Joseph Terrefort. It has taken me such a long time to uncover something he succeeds so well in hiding. Now my vigil has become a bond between us. I wait and watch and listen, and only when that little whistle stops do I doze off into a sleep that is no longer mine, but his, or eventually perhaps from day to day, thanks to this secret which he will soon be reading, ours at last.

Is that what they mean, I wonder, in those love-songs, when they talk of 'sleeping together'?

And if on stormy evenings the wind drives down from the hills, if a piercing winter wind suddenly veers round, I keep my eyes open for a gesture, a look of distress, of fear. But Joseph Terrefort merely lowers his head slightly. I know he is checking his breathing. He quickens his steps, pretends to smile at this unprovoked attack and absorbs the air in irregular gulps. Then he will take ten or twelve paces all on one breath.

And I am there close to him, listening every night, while he thinks I am asleep. Already that very first evening when we found ourselves sleeping side by side in the dormitory, I was listening to him. His heart was beating in my ears. I had slipped his pencil-case underneath my pillow. He had thought this an amusing idea and had done the same with the pencil-case I had given him in exchange. The breathing of my first friend intrigued me. It was like a continuous far-away sobbing. Already that little whistling sound. Like a cry for help.

At the start of this year when Sandro's boat capsized, when Joseph Terrefort leapt from his bed calling the name of our friend, the very first cry came from his nose, like a groan, a furious expiration of his whole being. This is the setting I choose for this impossible portrait: low clouds, a sea trembling with foam, the dark hull of a capsized boat tossed about by the waves. And those rocks against which our repeated shouts were shattered. Sandro had said to us: '*Non so dove andiamo. Ma quando lei mi guarda, so dove siamo.*' I don't know where we're going, but when you look at me, I know where we are. Perhaps there is no secret *malaise* in Joseph Terrefort. It may be quite a simple problem, a general feeling of oppression. Or is all this merely the expression of my desire to lose myself in him?

But the whistle still remains, and that distinguished nose dominating every glance. And when I make the inventory of his body, when my head nestles against the nape of his neck, when I am coiled over his belly, when I press his feet against my lips, suddenly I am breathless, almost gasping for breath and my heart is thumping. As if I were being robbed of my oxygen. Then I slide back to his face. I have to hear him breathing before I can recover. Joseph Terrefort smiles at me as if I had returned from a long journey. Can our complicity take us any further than this?

At Saint-Pardom there are only two odours he can tolerate, the flower-scented polish on the furniture or the parquet flooring, and the neutral smell of the books which, when they are new, he always insists on being the first to read. That is Joseph all over. This is your portrait.

And this is our life. More than a game, don't you think? When you have perused these lines, I shall have read the ones you have destined for me. Let us not laugh or still less smile at them. We still have so many, many things to learn about each other.

This deep-seated *malaise*, perhaps it is only I lurking inside you, devouring you. Yes, I breathe you in and sap your strength. Don't hold it against me. When I stretch out beside you, I do not in fact go to sleep. I play dead, that's all. Just doing my apprenticeship? With you.

# Third day

This text is my salvation. Here from these words I draw nourishment. It is like a magnificent repast at which I pretend to have facing me the guest of a lifetime. The great table of words is laid. That one empty place makes it seem like a banquet. Who else, between the sorbet and the *glacé* fruits, can rise to his feet but I, to make the speech which should in theory save mankind? What is dying in us and with us, Joseph, is perhaps life at its truest. To deride us they will accuse us of being dilettante. Let the sarcastic keep their sarcasm to themselves.

We were reunited just now at your place, at Saint-Pardom, after the ceremony. Clothilde wears her mourning for you in sober manner. A black cotton dress slightly too large for her, doubtless borrowed from a friend or neighbour. My wife Sabine's dress on the other hand was not without surprise. Nigger-brown taffeta with sleeves and collar trimmed with black lace. Where the devil did she dig that up, a rig-out I have never seen her wear before? It flashed through my mind that she'd had it run up by her dressmaker long ago, in order to look elegant on the day of our farewells. Like a first ball-dress.

There was your firstborn, your daughter Marie, who seems quite delighted with her studies in pharmacology at Bordeaux, and your son Pierre who has just passed his second year of medicine at Toulouse. There was also my son Henri, who has finally got rid of his southern accent in Paris and who talks about the polytechnic as if he had already been accepted at his coming entrance exam.

43

Sophie, my daughter, has arrived from Toulouse with your son Pierre, and says nothing about herself. Pierre is constantly trying to make her blush by quoting verses to her from *La Négresse Blonde*. She sat at your piano when we passed into the drawing-room and tried out the piece set for her exam at the end of the year at the Conservatoire. *La Campanella* by Paganini. Empty virtuoso music. My son, your godson, feeling jealous, took his turn at the piano and played *La Cathédrale Engloutie*. Debussy murdered with panache!

And if I run through the list of all those who are close to us, the reason may well be because we did not feel close enough to them, not because we were selfish but out of respect for each other since we were so rarely together. In the silence of this house, Joseph, where we most often took refuge when our wives and children were living together in my home at Copeyne, I have suddenly been struck by the thought of how we have multiplied ourselves. Thanks to the fertility of these two sisters, Sabine and Clothilde, we have inherited in our sons and daughters a great responsibility. Here we are about to cast into the world a future polytechnician, a budding doctor, a pharmacologist and a pianist, in all four of whom Sabine has cultivated an official feeling of respect for us, but unofficially contempt. Our little world shares the ambitious nature of my wife. And our children will have children and so *ad infinitum* in this overturning world.

On our way back from the cemetery, we walked along the Boulevard de Gesles. At the moment it is being tarmacked. What thick black smoke and what a smell of burning! Is there really any need to give up paving stones?

Shortly after coffee Pierre suggested a game of tennis. 'While we're here,' he said, 'we might as well take full advantage of it.' A nonchalance I make a point of reporting because I know how much it will appeal to you. Who knows if in some way Pierre will take after us a little? But his sense of humour does not lie very deep nor always ring true. When Pierre cracks a joke, he is running away from himself.

So I quickly came back to Copeyne. I left Saint-Pardom through the gate of the kitchen-garden, the one we would use when we were still afraid of village gossip, that same summer as the portraits; then I followed along by the big brook, red with blood because it was a Thursday, the day the butcher does his slaughtering. I walked past the wash-house and up again to my house along the fig-tree path, to my study, the place where I can find you again. The third day with you and without you! Oh, let this agony inspire me! Let me go on feeling these blows! But let there be no embellishment, nothing to throw me off course. There is no song of life without the obvious presence of death. Let there be no counterfeit echoes of this torment!

What follows, in line with what has gone before, must be a record of the facts. The body of our 'creative works' exists no more. Did it ever, when we were in such haste to tear up the poems we wrote to each other and destroy all written evidence of something that in fact could never be transcribed: the simple harmony of two human beings?

This text will confine itself to the periphery of our dual relationship, a zone of dry grasses that become fresh and tender, then change to fern and brambles and trees that grow taller and taller until they attain the height of the admirable elm, majestic. Yes I shall have to circle about us, using these few notes or letters which we first snatched then hid from one another, saving them from destruction not because they were the best, but because they were intimate moments not intended for close scrutiny. This undated letter from you, for example, waiting on my desk to be classified, a sad frustrated letter at the bottom of which you wrote: 'Never mind, I shall still be alive a year from now and so will you.' When did you write that? It must have been a long time ago. Jealously I kept that tiny fragment of paper, neatly pressed into three folds lengthways with my nail, for the strength of your conviction.

And in this world where everything is turned into a show, all glitter and brass, or as you would say titivated up, in an age in which poets create nothing but ghettoes where they enjoy denigration and destruction on the pretext of adding a fresh imaginative gloss to realism, at such a juncture in time I shall try to uncover that eternal layer beneath the skin which is woven out of sentiment, without which nothing can be truthfully expressed.

I am far from ignoring the risks of the undertaking. But if it can help me to live on after you, we shall give entire expression to ourselves within the pages of this notebook where I shall calligraphically set down all the evidence that speaks for the individual and much derided Nature. Our intelligence will never be equal to the instinct of an evergreen oak which sends out its roots, grows up straight with acknowledgements all round, increases its girth and its height, and unifies with everything about it.

And if your portrait makes me out to be a rustic fool, I should like to contribute one detail which defines me and amused you that day we swapped our pencil-cases, the day it all seemed to start. I am left-handed as you know. How many times was I given fifty, a hundred or even five hundred lines to write out with my right hand as a punishment? Our good Fathers deform you the better to form you. What an idea! But when on the first day of school we sat side by side on the same bench, when the teacher told us to open our exercise books, I opened mine back to front, on the last page. You burst out laughing. And got ticked off for it. You were told you weren't allowed to laugh! And I could not understand what had triggered you off or provoked the riposte. We had just entered the prison of civilized behaviour. Only when I saw you open your own book, red with shame, did I understand what one had to do if one wanted to be accepted. You knew already. I did not. It was my first exercise book. I wanted to start it by writing on the last page, then the one before the last and so on. Oddly enough, that is what I am doing today, with the notebook of our life, working back to front. So we shall be leaving each other with the same impression we had at our first meeting.

In the portrait I drew of you there is one thing missing too, something I did not then esteem to be essential: the extraordinary hardness of your body, the softness of your skin, the way your smile reflects the expression in your eyes, the precision of your gestures, your calm refusal to be hurried. To define you even better today at a time when you are deserting me, now that I am older I would say that everything about you was meticulous, from the look in your eyes to your caresses, even to the deference you would show when you had to acknowledge this or that inhabitant of our town.

But how in God's name can I complete this portrait when our joint creation can only be partially reconstructed here and will give the merest hint of what we are? I hope its incompleteness will make these everyday details all the more welcome.

Yes, you leave me feeling much older, whereas without thinking we never stopped seeing ourselves the way we were at Cazauban for example, or when Sandro brought us together, forcing us into collision through the clashing of our flesh.

I have already noted down a few headings for the chapters to follow this one, written on the third day: 'The Silver Dagger', 'The Rainbow', 'The Moonfishers', 'Tityre the Cat' and a few others of my invention or of yours. What does it matter when we always listened so attentively to one another? I shall just mention the date, whether you or I wrote it and the heading. That is all.

And in this notebook one thing will grow out of another. Now I shall do as you wrote to me in your letter of appeal, the first one I copied out, and take my time with time, whereas all the literature of today has been denied its liturgy.

47

Sabine has come in. I heard her sharp footsteps on the staircase. Then in the first-floor passage. She came and stood outside my study door. She listened for a moment. I was reading out loud what I had just written down: '. . . its liturgy'. She knocked and without waiting for an answer opened the door, saw that I was alone and simply asked: 'Who are you talking to?' Then she closed the door behind her. A bit too loudly for my taste. But that's the way she is. Perhaps she wanted me to admire her beautiful dress again, the one she won't wear a second time until it's in honour of me.

When you read the portrait I had just penned, you stood up and flung open the french windows of the drawing-room at Saint-Pardom. It was night. The August wind swept in, chasing away the delicate perfume of polish and bringing with it the strong odours of the night, of thick foliage and black felt, as when the town worthies are reluctant to go home and, as they leave the Café du Commerce, go on talking socialism. That evening you told me that your *malaise* was not of the body. It was beyond analysis, it came from everyone and everything around. 'It's the illness of a man too anxious to use his intelligence in pursuit of his own perdition.' I remember how you said 'per-di-tion', separating the three syllables very clearly, so that it suddenly made a threefold impression on me.

Then slowly you walked back to me. I was sitting with my head down, leaning forward, my elbows on my knees, my hands clasped together. You stood in front of me for a long time. I felt your hands flatten over my ears and grip me to lift me up. Facing me, with my head in your vice-like hands, you wiped my eyes with your thumbs. Two heavy stinging tears that refused to flow. Afraid that I had written too much, I had a feeling of sacrilege. And you whispered: 'Crying now?' I threw myself against you and we clung to each other as if we were both broken men. And in a deeper voice you said with a smile: 'That's not like you', which was followed by, 'But it's us all over.' I can see all that now and live it again with a clarity as startling as in one of those talking films which are all the rage just now and about which you said at the start of this new year: 'That's all we needed, a new cult like that. The churches will empty and those darkened halls will be full. All sorts of new desires will be created!'

But now I must report the outstanding event of this third day: the presence at the cemetery, but only at the cemetery for he was not at the cathedral for the funeral service, of Martial. Alone, without his wife, taller and broader, almost bloated with life. He kept a little apart, with his arms crossed waist-high and holding his cap as though he wanted to hide his private parts behind his headgear. That was how he stood there, the little rogue in our flesh. Discreetly. No doubt he was anxious to be present as much for your sake as for mine. I observed him. He never dared look at your coffin, not for one moment, but he followed every movement of mine. Sabine noticed him and shot out: 'It's scandalous!' I must have answered, 'He's our tenant farmer, sweetheart.' She pursed her lips a little. 'Yes, *ours*. But not Joseph's. So why . . .?' This was neither the place nor the time for a quarrel. And I never quarrel with Sabine. Writing down the name I often call her at the moment, 'Yes, sweetheart . . .' 'No, sweetheart . . .', makes me realize what cruel irony there is in all this sweetness. Yet somehow that irony is full of tenderness, I hope. After all, the Bérard sisters were proud to marry us. And I shall really have to copy down, uncut, those other messages we wrote to each other at the time we got married. The very same day. All four of us!

Yes, Martial, our wild boy, our war orphan, our protégé, our friend, thanks to whom we passed into adulthood and grew older; there he was all grown up, bald and unrecognizable, his face running with sweat. Or was it fear? He came, Joseph! I must look out his letters too, when he was a soldier. His way of writing was as much like yours as mine after the ceaseless labour of love we put into teaching him his alphabet, then his vocabulary and conjugations and punctuation, until the war snatched him away from us and turned him into a distant stranger. He was there. Unrecognizable. He had certainly put on his beautiful suit. The only one he has. The one he never wears. The one we gave him so that he could look smart on his wedding day. One of your suits, or was it one of mine? I don't know any more! Only one thing I remember: after the Armistice he had lost no time finding a bride. He came to announce it to us. And simply to ask us for a suit, the one he was wearing today. So there's Martial too, he mustn't be left out.

It's getting late. Night is falling. There's a sudden scent of geraniums wafting in from the terrace. What an infuriating smell. But Sabine is so fond of those flowers. No doubt she once detected that this is the only flower among so many that really upsets you, so potent is the scent it propagates at nightfall. And this year, even more than most, all the urns round the house at Copeyne are tumbling with those heady perfume-makers. And when the sun, after licking round them all day long, finally dips down, they exhale and disseminate their odour. And remind me of you. For two pins I'd let them stifle me too.

Through the window I can see a shadowy shape in outline against the darkness of the night, a corner of the roof of Saint-Pardom. And on the horizon the steeples of the Cathedral of Saint-Pierre and the Chapel of the Carmelites, and the foliage of the promenade. The first evening is falling asleep over your tomb, Joseph, as though it wanted to soften the fiery light of day, expunge the blackness of the dresses, rob Martial of his cap, and instruct the winds to rush in and sweep all the existing planes and surfaces away, while you install yourself in me and tell me for one last time to take good care of you. Care of us.

Thirty-two days of agony! I counted them, those days when Dr Berthollet, the Brigand's successor, contented himself with a late call to repeat that there was no hope for you and perhaps a little morphine . . . And that gesture you made with your hand, the palm toward us and the fingers stretched out, as if you were suddenly imbued with a vehemence to refuse any kind of injection when they were already bringing the syringe and the saucepan of boiling water from the kitchens and the Doctor was getting everything ready. No, no dreaming death for you. And with a look you begged Clothilde to leave us alone together once more. And I started reading to you again. Always in that Latin which filled us with so much pride and the grim determination to defend ourselves. *In medium quaerebant, ipsaque tellus omnis liberus, nullo poscente, ferebat* . . . The crops were gathered in common store and the earth gave its full yield of its own accord, freely and without constraint. Between us it was a *living* language, which purified the air until your very last breath.

And everything that we had read and reread throughout our life together came to me during that long agony of reading with a poignant new meaning, curiously revivified. Sometimes, with a different gesture, you would ask me to read a certain passage again. The one from Livy for example: the defeat and death of Hasdrubal. To mention the names of Marcus Livius or Lucius Portius was to gather round your bedside heroes, friends and witnesses of every kind. What a battle!

And if occasionally a hesitation in my voice betrayed my sorrow, a slight smile would flicker over your lips and as quickly fade. Then I would hear that little whistle in your breathing all the more acutely as it drilled more keenly through you. You were choking, that is all. Thus you were born, choking. And today I almost wonder whether it is not the same for any human being entirely ruled by integrity and desire, the crazy few on whom the laws of men no longer have a hold and who aspire to live against the common grain.

And the longer I went on reading, the more the content of my words seemed to reanimate you and prolong your agony. Sometimes, when you detected in my voice something that betrayed my anxiety at making you suffer, you would motion me to continue with a slight signal of your hand. You looked at me, Joseph, how you looked at me! The same look you used to give me when you were ahead of me and anxiously turned around to see if I was following you all right.

A noise on the terrace. Clothilde and our children have just arrived. Henri wants to introduce his fiancée, Jeanne. Already! Henri is calling me. We lunched at Saint-Pardom. We shall dine at Copeyne. You see, I shall never really know which of these two houses was ours.

And you will be here with me, within me, watching them forget you already. They are laughing. And I can hear them. A laughter that I know you accept. A puff of wind has passed. And blown away. And I am trying to capture it.

Sabine is intending to go to Paris and to stay there in the event of Henri passing his examination. Nothing counts for her except this son who is a stranger to me. This time they are all calling me in chorus. I must leave you.

# 27 September 1906. From Joseph.
## The silver dagger

Thirty men have come from Spain for the grape harvest. Robert, the tenant-farmer of La Sarriete, asked me to go. 'They're a rough lot,' he told me, 'and I fear the worst.'

When we arrived, Roland and I, a dust-laden wind gusted through the archway to the courtyard of the farm, as though it wanted to propel us inside. A dry stinging wind. My straw hat blew off. The men sitting in the shade of the surrounding walls all laughed. Then they stood up. Roland wanted to run after my hat. I stopped him and held on to his wrist for quite a while, forgetting that we were not on our own. Oddly enough this gesture imposed silence on the men. A suggestion of toughness?

Then Robert came into the middle of the yard to meet us. A young kid about five goes and picks up the hat and as he runs up to us, happily unclothed, he holds it out to me, laughing. 'This is Martial, my eldest!' Robert leans his weight on his son's head, as if the child had sprung from the palm of his hand! And while we observe him, the young boy covers his sex with his hand. I put my hat back on. Roland undoes the collar of his shirt. Robert beckons us to follow him.

In the common-room of the farm, one large table in the centre with a chair on one side and two chairs at either end. Robert advises us to sit down at each end of the table. Where are his wife and mother and his two daughters? A creaking board on the first floor of the farm indicates that they are hidden away. Robert motions to Martial to stay in the courtyard. 'Or go and get dressed.' The child says 'No!' Placing a bottle of plum brandy on the table, Robert looks hard at his son, playing the ogre to frighten him. Little Martial bursts into a second laughing 'No!' and rushes off into the wind. Robert closes the door.

'The wind was drying out our grapes. We had to do something quickly.' Robert pours us out a measure and we all clink glasses. But neither Roland nor I drink any of the bitter spirit. Robert has downed his glass in one and stares at us, astonished. 'If you don't drink, Monsieur Joseph, there's no friendship here. And you, Monsieur Raillac?' Roland is the first to respond, at one gulp too, letting out a great rasping 'Ah!' I drink in my turn, in nervous little sips, pulling a string of faces. For friendship's sake. I make them laugh. The only alcohol I like is the rich amber blood of our region. I like to cup the glass in the palms of my hands, roll the liquor around to warm it and then drink it in courageous little sips. I explain this to Robert. Roland asks for more and clinks glasses again. Which pleases our host. 'Twice is not too much, you should see the Spaniards. Every country has to go one better!'

Robert opens the door and signals to the men to enter. Then he takes his seat between us, excusing himself and calling us 'Monsieur' again. It appears that my mother used to come every year for what is considered to be something of a ceremony. And according to Robert the performance intimidated her in no way at all. Unless it were that the presence of a woman put the fear of God into the Spaniards and their leader, 'El Col'!

Ritual: the men file in and line up along the wall opposite Robert. I look at Roland. He lowers his eyes. We both feel stiff and starchy and suddenly, barely a league away from Saint-Pardom, pretty much like townies. Or is it because of the role of landlord that Robert has cast me to play, seated at one end of the table like a judge?

The last man enters and slams the door behind him. This is 'El

Col'. He picks up a chair, greets us with a nod and goes to sit down opposite Robert. Behind him his men are ranged like soldiers at ease, feet apart, arms hanging loosely at their sides. Their eyes converge on the drawer in the great table, which Robert slowly opens, glancing at us on his right and his left, as if he were afraid we might miss the best part of the show. First he takes from the drawer a large pistol, which he loads and sets down in front of him with the barrel facing 'El Col'.

In answer to this, 'El Col' pulls a long silver dagger from his belt and with one bold gesture drives it straight in under the table, the handle still within reach of his left hand. The men laugh. 'El Col' motions them to keep quiet.

Then Robert silently pulls from the drawer a large sheet of paper bearing a list of names, and a bag full of coins that he scatters over the table. He carefully folds up the bag and puts it back in the drawer which he presses shut with the tips of his fingers as he bends forward and pulls his chair up closer. Then he counts the coins and arranges them neatly in piles. Quite a pause for silent observation. The floorboards above have stopped creaking. Twenty-nine little columns, all the same height, and Robert gathers the remaining coins in the palm of his hand and slides it flat over the table towards 'El Col' who, without counting them, smartly pockets them.

Then follows the roll-call. At each name, 'Pedro Garcia Ripoll', 'Antonio Vasquez Tarrebo', 'Javier Rivera Angulo', a man approaches and makes a cross against his name where Robert points his finger, under the watchful eye of their leader. One false move and Robert would seize his pistol, 'El Col' would brandish his dagger. They would murder each other. Trying to reconstruct this scene reminds me of the underlying sense of drama, the macho challenge in it: putting themselves to the test, proving their virility. To whom?

Behind the door, his hands flattened against the glass, Martial is watching round-eyed, as if he too had been forewarned of danger. There he is, a little lad fascinated by the shadowy hall and the staring eyes of those silent men, with their rough beards, their hands stained as if scarred by the purple of the grapes, who approach one by one, make their mark, pocket the money and then retire.

When they had all had their turn and there was no more money on the table, Robert and 'El Col', at precisely the same moment, their eyes fixed on each other, put their weapons away. The pistol in the drawer. The silver dagger in the head man's belt. Without a word 'El Col' stands up. No expression on his face. He signals to his men to go. Martial vanishes from behind the glass like a little imp. One by one, heads held high, the men leave the room, blinking their eyes a little as if to accustom themselves once more to the crushing light which will guide them on the road for Spain, the homeward journey. Each man picks up his bundle in the shade of the high wall. And they all pass under the arched entrance to the farm without looking round, except for 'El Col' who waves to Martial standing on a hayrick and laughing as he shouts 'Adios'. 'El Col' waves to Martial, but not to us. We have no existence for these men. 'And that's how it is, Monsieur Joseph, every year. I know nothing about them except the crosses they make.'

It was only when I asked Robert why he was so insistent on our coming that he spoke in his true voice. A deep one with a musical intonation. 'Your mother,' he explains, 'used to come as the landowner. But you, you're different. It's not quite as if you're a stranger, but you don't belong here now.' And with a touch of amusement he recounts how a week before he had gone to a place near Marsolan in the early morning and got lost trying to find the farm of a certain Barzouille. He stopped to ask the way of some peasant working in a field. 'And do you know, Monsieur Joseph, how that scoundrel replied? If you don't know, you don't go!' Robert stared hard at me, then he smiled at Roland. 'And I felt even more lost than I had before. And after all that I came back from old Barzouille's place empty-handed. He wanted to sell me some stuck-up ganders my geese wouldn't have looked at twice. So, you see . . .'

We return to the common-room. Robert serves us another glass and this time we drink quite merrily. 'When those Spaniards cross the mountains, you'd think they carry the sunshine on their backs. I thought our vines would burst into flame!' With the help of the drink Robert's voice grows deeper and even more sing-song. Martial races into the room laughing and goes to perch on his father's knees, chewing on a piece of straw. Martial looks at me, then at Roland. He turns his face from right to left. Robert mutters: 'One day they'll stick a dagger in me. For the sake of a farthing. I used not to be scared at first. I thought it was just some kind of game. But from one grape-harvest to the next, I've been paying more attention to this silence. It's penetrating, Monsieur Joseph, Monsieur Raillac, a silence like that! It's silence clenching its teeth. And as they say, *en bocas cerradas no entran moscas*, a mouth that's shut keeps out the flies!' Martial understands and smiles. His father looks at him. 'And what about this one, who won't hear of going to school! This isn't my home any more, it's his! Sorry, Monsieur Joseph, I mean it's yours!' I believe I blushed. Like a kid. Like Martial, who was watching me anxiously just then. Robert explains: 'It's Martial who rules the roost round here. He's right of course, because outside this place, everything is foreign! Nothing but foreigners! It's all right, my liqueur, isn't it? So here's to friendship!'

We are going. Martial ahead of us, stark naked, with his hands clasped behind his back. 'They arrive, Monsieur Joseph, and they never say a word. They get on with their work and they leave again. Spiteful gossip has it that they kill all the cats they find and that's the only thing they eat. It may be true. In the last few weeks three of my cats have disappeared.' Martial stops at the archway, tugs at my hand and standing on tiptoe shows that he wants me to bend down. He gives me a kiss. He is however intimidated by Roland. Robert teases his son and explains that what you do for one person you must do for the other. Martial performs. I believe

57

we all laughed, Robert, Roland and I. Martial shrugs his shoulders.

Yes, we are all foreigners, ready to stab one another. Were it not for the kiss of a naked child. A straw in the wind!

The most dramatic experiences lie outside drama. The real theatre, without its *coups de théâtre*, is the theatre of life, when one observes it and listens intently. To die for the sake of a farthing.

# 20 June 1905. From Joseph.
## The rainbow

Today's newspaper, *La Dépêche*, has made a great fuss about the French motor-car trials for the Gordon-Bennett Cup, which were won by Théry and Muller, his mechanic, in a Richard-Brasier. The event took place in the Auvergne apparently over very difficult terrain. The 547 kilometres were covered in seven hours and thirty-four minutes at a speed of seventy-two kilometres an hour. So this is what excites people, and excites me too since I read it and lend sufficient importance to it to quote it in introduction to this note, which is the record of other real happenings, those that map out Roland's life and mine.

But there is a further reason to explain this place of honour: Gordon, Bennett, Théry, Muller, Richard, Brasier, this string of unknown names suddenly glorified in the headlines of a newspaper. Beneath it all lies the desire to create a sensation, in this case by moving faster, ever faster. What is the century which we have just entered? Reluctantly, without doubt, since the following events which Roland and I have lived through could lead to our being considered completely mad.

It rained yesterday, right at the end of the afternoon. One of those storms that seem to be trying to rip the leaves from the trees, when the wind plays at being a tornado while the rain scourges you and in exasperation turns to hail. Roland and I were returning from Polignac, one of the farms that have been neglected. Roland likes to see a farm abandoned for a while, as he claims that at a time when we have no special need of it, the land needs a period of rest

59

to become more fertile. The conversation we had on this subject will not be related here as Roland particularly dislikes admitting to the land-owning side of his character. That's the Political Science streak in him. I have no doubt he would have made an astute diplomat as he positively excels in the art of prevarication. He disguises the truth with a smile. He feigns ignorance of the fact that those few parcels of land which were not confiscated by the lackeys of the Second Empire during the trial of his blessed bell-ringing father are still considered accursed three or four decades later by those tenant-farmers whose job it should be to exploit them. Just think of it! Land that once belonged to a convict from Cayenne! So Polignac basks in its nettles and its scrubland. They even say that it has become a refuge for snakes and a playground for small game. I am writing this for Roland's sake, yes, for you my friend, so that if ever you read this you will know that I have not been taken in by your conceits. Some of them seem to me at times ill-considered. Not because this one leads to loss of income but because it is a kind of betrayal; for land needs to be worked and it breathes through its furrows. There I go again, worrying about breathing. Make fun of me if you like!

That storm has been tracking us down. We have watched it prowling, growling, louring as if the clouds had wanted to violate our earth without bursting. Here and there they would shred off into strips and disperse over the fields. Then a heavy wind got up, signifying a break, as if the earth in retaliation was either rejecting their advances or calling down the rain, for one never knows if the wind is an ally of earth or sky. Roland took me by the hand. A gesture that really belongs to me when, out of breath during our long excursions, I feel the need to be guided, to hold on to something, to let myself be led. A gesture that would seem laughable to the average man but is in fact quite straightforward and generally accepted by your Sicilians for example. Sandro used to take us by the hand each in turn. That was the gesture which shaped our alliance.

Then the rain begins to fall in isolated swollen drops. The quicker we walk, the faster and more driving the rain. We take shelter on high ground, standing pressed against the wall of the shrine of Saint-Jacques, protected by the overhanging roof from the curtain of rain falling in front of us.

'Do you know how rain tastes?' asks Roland. I shake my head. He lets go of my hand, grips the back of my neck and kisses me. 'That's how!' And he laughs. Then I remember inhaling the combined smell of our sodden hair and the stones of the building we were sheltering under. Roland is humming some wild invented tune, with his lips half open and his teeth clenched, hoarse, like a war-cry that fails to emerge from his throat. 'And do you know how damp earth tastes?' And he starts kissing me again. 'Oh yes! . . . Oh yes! . . .'he shouts, as he removes his grey jacket and his white shirt. 'I'm crazy, I know!' He takes off his trousers, his underclothes, his shoes and his socks and lays them in a bundle next to the wall. 'Come on!' I don't move. 'But that's just why! *Everyone* can see us!' He walks a few paces in the rain, arms outstretched to the sky. I can see the arching shoulders, the hollow in the small of his back, the rain pouring over his body. He starts rubbing himself all over. He turns. 'Come on! If you don't, you'll be struck by lightning!'

We used to play these games as children. But this time Roland takes me by surprise. Since our trip to Italy we have been in the habit of limiting the scene of our reunions to the four walls of our bedroom. They give us protection from prying eyes. Now suddenly Roland is off again. He is rushing at me. We fight. As I push him back, he bumps his temple against the wall. A bead of blood bubbles up. I try to say I'm sorry. 'No, get your clothes off!' And he moves away, singing out 'Hurry up!'

As I write them down, these cries strike me like blows and turn into an appeal for help. I roll my clothes into a ball and put them on top of his, as though in this situation the protective role was mine. The way I look at Roland must resemble the quizzical look of every imaginable peeping Tom or muckraker who goes off into the bush like us. I join him. The storm is rumbling on and the rain becomes surprisingly warm as it lashes at us. Roland throws me down on the grass and playfully pretends he is going to jump on me. I catch hold of his foot. He falls flat. Holding his wrists still, I pin him to the ground and lie on top of him. 'Bravo!' he cries. He tries to wriggle away, but gives up and laughingly shouts: 'Spit . . . go on, spit at me!'

He looks up and grins: 'Coward! What are you waiting for?' Stomach to stomach, with my thighs glued to his, our feet hooked together, our crossed swords pressed into our bellies, my arm outstretched to grip his wrists and my chest raised, with his smiling head twisting to right and left, I spit all over his face, my mucus mingling with the rain. Holding his head still, he suddenly gazes at me, serious and surprised. He lifts himself up a little and spits straight at my face in turn, before releasing himself with one bound, rolling in the grass, standing up and running off down the hill with his arms flung out at his sides, welcoming the sky, the rain and the thunderclaps.

I remained lying where I was. Astonished. Without realizing, I had just ejaculated. Shot all over my stomach and my face. Nothing behaves more unexpectedly than one body in confrontation with another when the combat is sparked by desire. We shall never learn too fast how to shake off our taboos, our standards of normality. Once a couple has come into being it spins off on its own and answers no accepted codes of conduct. What Roland asked me to do will alter our relationship once again, just as reading his portrait of me has altered the way we spend our nights. What were once only parallel patterns of sleep were eventually to become mutual listening sessions, for from that time on we have been observing each other without admitting it, and thanks to the exchange of each other's writings we have learnt to acknowledge all those things we exchange and share during the fitful passage of the night.

I wipe the rain and the saliva from my face and go to join Roland.

We sit down on the grass side by side, elbows on knees, with our hands folded, contemplating the same landscape in silence. Are we taking stock, under the churning sky, the drifting clouds, the tumultuous flashes, the rumbling and the harrying lashes of rain, of all those things that separate us still and of all those discoveries we still can make to bring us closer together? The one great offence is the refusal of love in its totality. Roland mutters: 'We'd better not stay under a tree.' Almost at the same moment, less than half a league away, the lightning strikes a young oak, which bursts into flames and then, being wet, as quickly consumes itself in black smoke, a sinuous column that rises to the clouds and darkens them. To us it all seems quite normal, for people always think lightning strikes elsewhere.

In three days I shall be twenty-eight. Roland and I are reaching a watershed. Perhaps we are like Théry and Muller at the wheel of their Richard-Brasier. We are becoming more proficient in wearing out the machinery of our bodies in order to break records. But that is an exploit which concerns no one but us. May this text be our version of *La Dépêche*, which takes as its scoop for the day the story of a storm with two tenebrous characters spitting at each other. It would be unacceptable to admit that these writings stem from us, this social microcosm for two which regulates our lives. Every one of these lines is a complete work in itself. I am at one and the same time author, editor and printer, and all I need is one reader. Each line is a single edition dedicated, Roland, to you. And you will not read this text yet, never read it perhaps, because I shall hide it away. Unless I leave you first, in which case I shall bequeath it to you, together with all those others I have already concealed and will go on concealing, in order to help you to reconstruct the events of our life. Only then perhaps will you decide to turn your mind to others and tell them of our existence, even at the risk of seeing ourselves abused and accused of all kinds of romantic nonsense, when the real truth about us lies in the coupling of our bodies.

The body, which belongs to matter, contains all the gentleness and violence of our thoughts, the ultimate arena of all our interplay, the territory through which we must and should pass, in a century ruled by the new broom and the money bag, if we want to give all that up and live.

The rain is growing more capricious, at times whipping us, then it hesitantly slants away, eases off and then lashes us again. I think we are beginning to get cold, sitting next to one another like this, listening giddily to our own silence, in stunned exhilaration to think we had spat at each other. Every orgasm is an expectoration! That anything is dirty or filthy is an unnatural notion that hampers a wholehearted embrace. How long have we remained like this, staring at the oak that was sacrificed in the ritual of the storm, and down below at the fields and the paths and the hedgerows, all the natural architecture of a thirsty land that drinks what is offered without questioning whether it is good or bad, virtuous or wicked, done or not done. Our expectorations were our kind of thunder and lightning, a threat. A kiss.

When the rain has stopped for good and the clouds are breaking up, Roland turns to me, rests his chin on my shoulder and looks at me with a smile. 'Understand?' he asks. Then he laughs. The sun begins to come out, its rays darting here and there, piercing the clouds and planting themselves in the earth like the columns of a temple to welcome us. A rainbow forms. 'Look where it springs,' murmurs Roland. And he points to a clump of trees on the left and moves his finger round in a semi-circle until it indicates the top of a hillock. Between these two points lie meadows, a stream, a cornfield, a cliff topped by a ruin and the burnt-out oak.

His chin is bruising my shoulder. Roland pivots round, stretches out and rests his head in the hollow between my thighs and my stomach, looking up vertically at me. I shift to one side, resting on my elbows, my hands flat on the water-soaked grass. A curious sensation, rain drying on the surface of the skin, astringent, almost acid, as though it were going to leave burnt patches behind. And a disturbing presence, that creature in my crotch, like a birth. Roland looks at me. 'That rainbow is a gateway. Larger than any we have passed through. We each ought to start from either end, meet in the middle and open the gates. Take a good look where it starts and where it ends. As we get closer, it will have vanished.' Are those the precise words he used? The words, perhaps, but what is missing is the intonation, an almost aggressive tone of voice, for Roland seems to expel every word in haste. He jerks them out. Like a provocation. Roland leaps to his feet with one bound. 'Let's go!'

We quickly get dressed. Roland wipes my stomach clean with the tail of his shirt, calling me a little pig. He talks. He boasts: 'I came too, after you. With my back to you and my arms spread wide. It was gone with the wind. No need to touch myself. The clouds were licking me.'

We walk downhill, slithering over the grass, avoiding the muddy paths scored with puddles. As the rainbow was fading at our approach, we had to make for our goals as quickly as possible. For me the clump of trees, for him the top of the hillock. And at a distance of about a hundred metres we wave to each other and advance slowly towards each other in a straight line. I cross a meadow. Roland passes close to the oak. Then I jump a hedge. Roland disappears behind the ruin. Another meadow, making straight for my friend. Roland reappears, then a sunken path, a short climb, thorn bushes, a smell of syringa and an impression that the brambles are trying to prevent me from rejoining this being who is a part of me, whose head lies cradled in my crotch, whose vertical gaze uplifts me to the sky, as if we were about to take wing. Then down again, a little valley, and Roland is not far off. I smile. The stream is exactly halfway between us. On the bank I take my shoes off and turn up my trouser-bottoms. On the opposite bank Roland does the same, and it is when our feet are in the storm-muddied waters that we meet to join hands, turn to face the East and open the great gates of the rainbow.

A few feet above us the trees are bending over our heads to make a tunnel of green, the water reaches up to our knees and we feel the ground dip beneath us, as if soon we would be out of our depth. I give Roland a push and we start swimming, fully dressed. Careless of everything, laughing at all those other people, we draw closer together in an activity, far more than a game, which expresses our determination to concede nothing and to persist in surprising one another. The water has a pungent taste, like saliva. The rainbow has just collapsed over us. And we laugh at the thought that we are still children. Nothing outlandish in all this. We are just bathing, that's all. Dripping wet, that's all. Just rejoicing in the fact that we have opened a great imaginary gateway and gone marching and swimming through the water in our mouths.

No poem could ever truly convey the harmonious orchestration of the smell of the rain, the rending of the lightning, the rolling of the thunder and the dark mountains of cloud, as if everything in the Heavens had conspired to petrify us for ever in our embrace.

We returned home wet, bare-chested, our shirts and jackets over our arms, our shoes in our hands. We met nobody on the way. Not until we reached Saint-Pardom, when we bumped into crazy old Mother Adeline leaving her house as usual in the evening to walk round the town singing her obscene songs. '*Qui vaï . . . qui vaï . . . li humen di amourousco . . .*' she shouted when she saw us. Then she started singing the same words to taunt us, in that language of hers which is neither the *langue d'oc* nor our own patois, but entirely of her own invention, concocted to create her own love songs. When she takes her evening stroll through the town, mothers call their children indoors and hide away their daughters, while the men playing bowls or on the café terraces make fun of the madwoman. 'You go on singing, Adeline, loud and clear, while I prime my weapon!'

With her hands on her hips, Adeline watches us go into Saint-Pardom. Her singing suddenly switched into a lower key. It sounded more like panting or a succession of barks. Roland took me by the arm. 'Don't look at her. She knows everything.

She has merged with someone's body too. And one never emerges intact!'

We built up a great wood fire in the drawing room. Our clothes were drying. Each in his armchair, hands laid flat on the arms, facing the fire with his legs outstretched, there we stayed until the logs turned to glowing embers, then to ashes.

Very late at night, when we had decided to go up to our room, Roland murmured: 'Literature is like an ember. You have only to blow on it. It's the reader who creates it. Read me! Write it! I felt you were living that rainbow in order to describe it. Come on . . .' Like a gash, that one in his temple, the one wound in a day I long to caress. 'It's nothing. Come on!' We go upstairs. I start writing. He's asleep already. No, he's waiting for me to join him. The gateway of the night. Different gates. There are so many entrances for us to take into the city we are building together.

# 7 September 1906. By me, Roland.
## The Moonfishers

The seventh day of our excursion. We cover two or sometimes three leagues a day. With bare feet in studded clogs, haversacks on our backs and trousers cut short at the calf, we are a subject of mirth to the inhabitants of the villages we pass through. They ask us what wares we are peddling or when the pantomime's going to start. We've been called by various nicknames: 'The mustachioed musketeers', 'The Tartarin trotters', or 'The *sans-culottes*!' Everywhere we give rise to laughter and bring pleasure to all. It is true that our style of dress, crowned with panama hats, is somewhat unusual, but it could also be that our identical travelling costume makes us look like ridiculous twin brothers who have both outgrown their clothes.

This great trip round our town is meant to last about eleven or twelve days. We decided to make it on foot and travel as light and unencumbered as possible. We had the idea of cutting our trousers to calf-length just before we set off, and as neither Joseph nor I have a servant at home we didn't even try to hem them. We cut them short, that's all. And the farther we walk, the more they fray into a fringe, so much so that one innkeeper drew my attention to the fact that they would make good fly-whisks.

We like to call this 'a trip round our town'. It is really quite a journey. We drew a circle on an ordinance survey map with our town at the centre, the radius being the distance our eyes could see as far as the horizon. So we are making a circular tour of everything that lies within the limits of our own patch of sky, either from Saint-Pardom or from Copeyne. And when we reached our starting point, which will also be our destination, didn't it amuse us to think that this was the place where we would find ourselves on the brink of the abyss?

Yesterday we got to Montestruc. A wedding party was in progress under the plane trees of the Grand-Place. On the terrace of the Cercle Républicain they were celebrating. We needed refreshment, but it was so crowded we started to walk away. The bridegroom caught sight of us, stood on his chair and called out to us: 'Hey, there, you two crackpots!' All the guests stared at us. And there we were, sharing their table. 'Where are you from?' 'Where are you going?' We answer evasively. 'We're walking.' 'Good Lord, they're walking!' No less than the bride herself serves us with drinks. It is three in the afternoon. That wedding breakfast will go on till evening. We have to stay. Every now and again Joseph looks at me and smiles. What can we do? Gradually we let the festivities take us over.

The whole village is there. Plus the close friends and acquaintances of the groom. And above all his cousins, the Bérard sisters: on several occasions he comes to whisper in our ear about them, as though they were the rarest of pearls. 'Over there, the two girls in rose-pink, they're the daughters of the owner of the local Bazaar . . .' I ought to write 'raouze' instead of 'rose'. What a difference his accent made to those words. Sorry, 'thaouze'! What a lot we lose when we try to slot all our words into identical grey boxes!

Then it was the musicians' turn. The bride and groom open the dance, awkwardly, to the accompaniment of applause and saucy remarks. We drink and clink glasses. The groom offers to lend us some trousers so that we can invite his cousins to dance. But we decline. We are anxious to leave. Joseph explains that we have a long way to go. The bridegroom replies: 'The road will wait . . .' And he grins almost conspiratorially to make us share fully in his enjoyment of it all.

69

The old men chew their tobacco, the women flutter their black fans, the children jump out at each other from under the tables, the dogs bark, the young ladies stick close to their mothers and the young blades lean up against the trees munching a twig of elder or smoking a cigarette. It will soon be time for the liqueurs. The bridegroom returns to the charge: 'Never mind. You go right ahead. My uncle and aunt know who you are and their daughters want to dance.' And once again we become the centre of attention. The musicians stop playing and whisper into each other's ears. We shake hands with Madame Bérard, owner and cashier at the Grand Bazaar, and then we courteously help the rose-clad young ladies to their feet, the perfect bridesmaids. Joseph jokingly presents himself in military fashion with a click of his heels. The musicians are playing a waltz for the four of us, just for us four, since we have once more become the attraction for everyone. This seems to amuse the Demoiselle Bérard whom Joseph is piloting, but not the one whose waist I am clasping and clumsily whirling round. The rhythm of that waltz is so slow and sluggish it is more like a *bourrée*. Without taking proper dance-steps, we just drag our feet round. It's a ridiculous spectacle but everyone seems pleased, except for my partner who is all blushes, red cheeks and rose-pink gown, with two little staring black eyes peering vaguely into the distance. I ask her her Christian name. 'Sabine . . .' she answers. And pulls a face. A very pretty face, for my chosen one, my demoiselle, is beautiful and knows it.

Then the lads who hadn't dared invite the Bérard sisters to dance, the bridegroom's younger brothers, Denis, Lalo, Etienne, and their friends from the village, Antoine, Albert and little Elie all throng round us as though we were heroes. 'They're too stuck-up, those two', 'Their parents only brought them to show them off', 'Serve them right if you trod on their toes'. Darkness suddenly falls. Old man Bérard goes off to fetch his motor-car. 'And he drives it at night too! Stirring the dust up all over the countryside!' Around the Bérards, formal leave-taking is under way. We shake hands with the parents. Their daughters lower their eyes. We catch the names Cayenne and Rigand coming from their lips.

70

From their mother, too, smiling at us, half-flattered, half-alarmed. 'Do come and call on us, we've never dared invite you.' Father Bérard proudly urges his lady to climb into their glossy machine. The bride joyfully explains that this is the first time a motor-car has stopped at Montestruc. 'And all because of me!'

But if today I want to make a note of yesterday's events, taking advantage of a short halt (Joseph has just dozed off on the grass with his head under a shady fern), it is not to recount what was in fact a common-or-garden wedding in our part of the world with a luncheon that finishes more like a dinner party or a late supper, dish after dish of fish, game and red meat with all the trimmings, not counting the cheeses and the thirteen desserts to choose from, but so that what happened next shall never be forgotten. When Denis, Lalo, Etienne, Antoine, Albert and little Elie refused to let us go back on the road, they all offered to put us up at their parents' place, or in a certain barn which, as they informed us, 'even Surrelac has used to roll his Jezebel in the hay'.

The musicians put their instruments away. The owner of the café issues orders for his tables to be taken in. His wife sweeps the square. A few old men remain on their chairs, their heads drooping over their chests, mulling over their memories in their sleep. The bridal pair have vanished as if by magic. The bride's mother comes to thank us for being the life and soul of the party and for dancing with her nieces, who 'were feeling out of things, because they were rather out of their element'. Joseph whispers in my ear: 'When we venture into the outside world, are we out of our element?' He smiles. 'Sorry, but I have had a drop to drink.'

And that is the main point about yesterday evening: intoxication and bogus *bonhomie*. The six young lads crowd round us, cracking jokes and thinking up all sorts of pranks, repeating again and again: 'It's not over yet, it hasn't finished, it's only just starting!' With all the lights out, their faces are sculpted by the brilliance of a clear moonlight night. They loosen their shirt collars. They point their fingers at the sky. 'He's going to stick it up the moon. That way they won't have any babies.' They laugh, their breath reeking of alcohol. Antoine, the oldest (is he even twenty?) and the coarsest as well, walks away from the group, rests his head against the trunk of a lime tree, clasps his hands behind his back, opens his mouth wide and vomits. Then he straightens up, wipes his lips and rejoins us with a broad grin. Belching. Little Elie is the only one to laugh. The rest look afraid that we might be offended, and again ask us not to desert them. 'Let's go for a swim!' And there we are, tagging along, seduced. Joseph is as thrilled by their company as I am. He avoids my eyes, just as I turn mine aside when he looks at me. One exchange of glances and we would be off and away!

We walk down a road to the river. The moonlight seems to get brighter and looks bluer too, or is it, I'm not sure, that our eyes have adjusted to it by now? All I can see is shadow upon shadow, the men clearly silhouetted against a halo of sky. We leave the village behind. Antoine stops, pulls a penknife from his jacket pocket and makes a neat incision in the palm of his hand. We look at him in surprise. He lifts his hand to his mouth to suck the blood and then holds his arm out to the moon, raises his head to the sky and staggering slightly, shouts: 'Now he's got her, he's having her now!' Joseph draws closer to me. I won't look at him. We have got to follow this encounter through to the end. Denis murmurs: 'Don't take any notice of him. He's in love with Hélène and she wouldn't take him because he's a butcher. His pockets are full of knives!'

Here they are, diving naked into the ice-cold waters of the Verse, yelling and screaming, splashing one another or ducking each other's heads under the water. 'Come on!' And we have joined in. They throw themselves into our arms, pretending to fight and wrestle with us and pull us out of our depth, all in fun, only in fun of course, but so that their bodies could slide against ours, while we furtively clutch at theirs. Even young Elie dives under and slides between my legs to pop out in front of Etienne, who is waving his clenched fists at me, laughing and threatening to

72

punch me. 'Makes you feel good, all this, doesn't it? Come on, put 'em up!'

Then we are out of the water. Etienne throws his arms round Elie. 'He's cold, he's shivering.' 'Give him a rub, he likes that.' Their laughter was clear, sharp, soul-piercing, harsh and weird. I shall have to rewrite all this, compose it properly. But how do you do that without elaborating? These words spring singly to my mind, bereft of syntax!

Standing naked on the river bank, our feet in the sharp blades of grass, the game is for us to slap one another and get warm, pinch one another's cheeks, shoulder each other out of the way, kick each other in the stomach. And laugh. Above all we roar with laughter. For it must never become too serious. 'Hélène, Hélène, here we come!' And they play at hitting one another with their pricks, thrusting their bellies forward, their hands clasped behind their necks, their bodies arched, lubricious little beasts. Antoine is proud of his phallus. But he never touches it. Nobody touches anybody's. Bodies brush in combat. That is all. Young Elie takes refuge in my arms. This time I exchange a glance with Joseph. He is smiling.

Then Lalo uncorks a demijohn and starts drinking from the bottle. The flask passes from hand to hand. Elie falls asleep, close up against me. No more shouting, no more games. We are sitting in a row with our feet in the water, looking at the river at rest, the reflection of the moon and, on the opposite bank, a field, a donkey, a coppice, then the woods, a hill, the night sky to the east.

The silence is shared between us. Eight of us, a number the locals dislike. A number that spells death. And hugging Elie closer, I feel a kind of presentiment. I want to make a sign to Joseph for us to leave, but he is gazing at Antoine, fascinated, or perhaps just curious.

They are drinking again and we drink with them. As I put my lips

73

to the neck of the bottle suddenly it is all of them I am kissing. This flask has become each of their mouths in turn, dispensing wine that is pungent and heavy. And once again I feel troubled. Albert throws the empty demijohn into the waters of the Verse. 'Our talisman!' The bottle floats, then sinks, swept away by the current. A few eddies, then the surface of the water regains its smoothness and the image of the moon is restored.

'Let's go fishing for the moon,' shouts Antoine. 'You're crazy!' 'You'll see!' And Antoine stands up, dives in and swims off towards the reflection. Disturbed, the image disappears. Then Antoine, as if alarmed, thrashes the water with his fists and flails around in a circle. 'Where is she? Where's she gone?' The others laugh. Young Elie wakes up and with a light shrug of the shoulders curls up again still closer to me. Antoine swims back to the bank. Albert and Etienne stretch out their hands to him, then let go. He drops back into the water. We choke with laughter. Then Antoine hauls himself out, shakes himself like a dog, one leg at a time, and then, wriggling his back, cries out, pointing first at the river then the moon: 'I nearly had her, I felt her slip between my fingers.' Antoine looks at the groom's three brothers and adds: 'You'll see what I'm going to give Hélène, your beautiful sister-in-law. The moon on a silver plate!'

The water is still again. The moon's reflection reappears, clear, distinct, inviting. Antoine tries to dive in again, but Etienne holds him back. 'It's not impossible, you know!' Antoine pushes Etienne to the ground. Lalo and Denis throw themselves on top of Antoine and pin him down. 'Keep still!' 'I can do it, I tell you, I can!' With a twist of his back Antoine frees himself, bounds off and dives in again head first, vanishing beneath the water as though he wanted to pluck the moon from below, to take her by surprise, his moon, his dream. And when his face re-emerges halfway across the river at the exact spot where the reflection had been, Antoine utters a hoarse cry and once again starts lashing at the water. He returns to the bank slowly and calmly, gliding back as if drifting with the current. As he comes out of the water, he mutters: 'I'll get her!' He sits down on his clothes with his head in his hands. He is either sobbing or spitting or belching again, no one is quite sure which, but he appears to be dribbling. He laughs. Silence. A long silence during which Lalo, Denis, Etienne, Albert, Joseph and myself all stare at one another. Time to go home, to split up as soon as we can. But it is a brutish silence. Antoine raises his head and once more sees the moon's reflection. He repeats: 'I know I can, I'll have her . . . Do you hear? I will have her!' Joseph stands up in order to get dressed. Antoine pulls out a knife hidden among his clothes and, brandishing it, yells: 'Stay where you are, stranger!' Lalo motions Joseph to sit down. We all stare at the moon and her reflection, at the flowing Verse. I can feel Elie's heart beating, so much more slowly than mine.

From the opposite bank the donkey seems to be watching us, taunting us. He moves down to the river, stretches out his neck and starts drinking. Ripples form in concentric circles that shiver the surface of the water and trouble the reflection of the moon. 'The bastard,' shouts Antoine, on his feet, knife in hand. Imperturbably the donkey drinks. Antoine turns to us and calls us to witness. 'He's stealing her from me. He's going to drink her!' Joseph moves nearer to me. Lalo smiles. Etienne stifles a laugh. Denis signals to them to keep still. Albert, with his head down, is pulling blades of grass up between his legs. Either he is trembling or he's cold. 'He's drinking my moon, I tell you, he's drinking my moon!' 'Stop it, Antoine, now that's enough . . .' 'What did you say?' Antoine goes up to Denis, picks him up by the scruff of the neck, hoists him like a sack and flings him to the ground. 'You're yellow, the whole lot of you, but you'll see what's what. He's drunk her, I tell you!' Antoine holds out an arm to indicate the troubled surface of the water, the effaced image of the moon and the donkey still quenching his thirst. 'This time I know where I can find her!'

For the third time Antoine dives in, his teeth clenched round the knife, and crosses the river. 'Come back!' 'Antoine!' We all shouted the same name. Just the one name. Automatically. I don't know why.

Antoine reaches the opposite bank. He approaches the donkey, which is still drinking, and sticks his knife in. Once, twice, ten times? At first I counted. How does a drunken butcher know how many blows he strikes? Denis simply said: 'Good thing it's a donkey and not a man. My brother warned us.' When I turned my eyes away Joseph ordered me to look. Antoine is disembowelling the animal. The carcass is lying on its side, its blood and guts sliding into the river. Antoine is raking about in it all, searching for his dream. Behind him, clear on the surface of the water, the image of the moon has taken shape again. And that was it.

On his knees, Antoine buries his arms and plunges his face into the disembowelled donkey. We, the spectators, watch from the opposite bank. Who said that spectators don't participate like actors? Antoine rises to his feet and looks across at us. Daubed with blood, he waves his fist at us. He pushes the donkey's carcass into the river, slithering over the intestines and righting himself. Then he crosses the field, turning his back on the moon and her reflection, and vanishes into the coppice, into the dark night to the east.

Albert is the first to get dressed. Then he takes Elie in his arms. Etienne has passed me my clothes. Lalo tries to laugh when Joseph steps into his cut-down trousers. The donkey's carcass has vanished, swept away by the waters of the Verse. One small patch of red on the opposite bank. And the moon, sinking already. Brief notes, but I must never rewrite them.

Joseph has just woken up. 'What are you doing?' 'Writing.' 'What?' 'Yesterday.' Joseph went back on the road without a word. I stay there alone, long enough to write these last few lines. Yesterday. Like today. Or tomorrow, if one goes on living. Cruelty is timeless.

As we were leaving the river bank, Antoine's clothes were still there. Denis said: 'What shall we do with them?' Albert answered: 'Leave them.' Lalo picked them up and explained with a laugh: 'No, it's more fun if I take them!' The day was dawning. Already.

Denis, Lalo, Etienne, Albert, Antoine and little Elie, I shall never forget those names. They are chained together. If ever I see the reflection of the moon again, the water will always turn to blood, like a violent hope sacrificed because it is unfulfilled. The three brothers went home together. We watched them walking away, hands in pockets, shoulders hunched, kicking at the stones. And I caught myself thinking how they too would have enjoyed beating the handsome bridegroom, their eldest brother, lucky devil! Albert took little Elie by the hand. The boy looked at me and asked: 'You'll come back?' I smiled and then I answered: 'Perhaps.' The lad turned to Albert with a shrug of the shoulders. 'That means they'll never come back!' They left us on our own in the deserted square. Joseph simply said: 'The things that go on within our own horizon!'

Good thing it was a donkey and not a man! On our way out of the village the shutters were flung open at the first-floor window of a house. A smile, a face: it was the bridegroom greeting the rising sun. He caught sight of us and made us a little gesture of collusion, turning round quietly towards the interior of the bedroom, as though Hélène should not on any account be wakened. *En route*!

# Seventh day

Here I am, Joseph, recomposing us with a hollow heart. These writings are neither yours nor mine, but ours, and in no other place do we still exist. It's as if we had been torn from one another in the first flush of an embrace that must have lasted almost forty years, the dramatic tragedy of a pencil-case which could have gone on unfolding still.

Our children have set off again, to Bordeaux, Toulouse and Paris. Henri is taking his examinations in a few days' time. Sabine reproaches me for not thinking enough about him. She has stopped watering the plants and the flowers and the trees in our park, as if she were determined to let everything die before we leave. Yesterday she turned out the attic. She sorted out, in her own words, all the old junk that's crying to be thrown away. With every gesture and every look she is making plans for the future. She often goes into town to visit our parents-in-law in the hope of extracting her share of the Bazaar: it costs money to go to Paris! Did we ever suspect, the day of the wedding at Montestruc, that six years later we would marry that blushing pair and that they would wait for so long before they won us round and decided to accept us? An odd sort of passion. But won us round to what? Isn't it really unpardonable that our children should be such strangers to us? They are *their* children, not *ours*, for they shaped them in the image that *they* desired. Not so much Clothilde as Sabine, of course. That first waltz set the measure. And I could not help being struck yesterday, as I copied the chapter on the Moonfishers, by those first reflections I made on the subject:

Clothilde delighted to be dancing with you, and Sabine already looking beyond it.

This morning I went to Saint-Pardom. For the first time since her marriage Clothilde was making a home for herself in this house which was always really *our* home. Sabine is watching her sister leave Copeyne not entirely without pleasure. 'After all, the children are grown up and from now on Clothilde should live with memories of the life she never lived.' I am quoting word for word exactly what my wife said, but omitting her smile, an ostensible sign of tender affection that only clumsily masked her delight. 'And now Copeyne is free, why not sell it!'

Clothilde wanted to talk to me. She took me straight into what used to be our bedroom. Our bed and your deathbed. She pulled the curtains, opened the windows and pushed the shutters back. 'This house needs to breathe again!' Yes, she said the word 'breathe'. She fixed me with a probing yet disarming look, as though inviting me to make a confession or admit some indiscretion. 'I'd like you to come here as often as possible, so you can go through all the cupboards and drawers and poke around everywhere. Because it's all so strange to me and it can never be mine.' No hard edge to her voice. Just a kind of doggedness. A gentle determination not to confront what her sister calls the 'memories of the life she never lived'. Then Clothilde went to the door of your study. She turned the handle thoughtfully, respectfully, and opened the door, beckoning me with a look to go inside, just as you often used to do, the same beckoning look on the very same spot. Clothilde will destroy nothing that is still alive.

In the library she explained to me that she wouldn't touch anything there, but that on the other hand she refused to live in a house with 'two dead rooms overhead'. Then her smile was I suppose meant to cover her emotion, because she murmured: 'I want it to be full of fresh air, light and sunshine.' And with the tips of her fingers she stroked your desk, leaving a bizarre pattern in the fine layer of dust that had already gathered on its leather surface. Did she want to spell out some word that only looked like a word, like one of those signs you used to trace on a misty window-pane or on the back of a piece of blotting-paper, inventing your own language like Adeline, keen as we all are to test out how dead our own living language really is or how terribly alive our dead language, Latin, was for us, when we spoke it in front of our wives, because we didn't want them to understand what we were saying? Only Clothilde had retained some knowledge of the humanities instilled into them by the Carmelite nuns. So it was an ignorance she feigned when she claimed not to understand our conversation, whereas in fact odd snatches of it revived her memory of some of the words once translated and engraved upon her mind and gave her some intimation of our secret. That is what she told me when she made that mark, that pattern on your desk. And it is thanks to that unknown word, suggested rather than transcribed, that I realized how much closer of the two sisters Clothilde was to us both. She used a panel from the skirt of her black dress to wipe away the mark she had made, apologizing for still being dressed in mourning when all your life you had been so scornful about those 'dreary masks of grief'. Thus, by her quiet, gentle, almost caressing voice and by the look in her eyes, Clothilde gave expression to many things that had their source in you, were you, as though she felt bound in this way to welcome me back to what had always been for me a kind of home from home.

Then, sitting at your desk and arranging according to size those pencils you always used to keep so well sharpened, she announced that Sabine had obtained from her parents the Bérards, 'so that Henri would be able to complete his studies to the best advantage', not only an important sum of money, a sort of bequest during their lifetime, but also and above all the assurance that she would inherit three-quarters of the estate, whereas Clothilde herself would only be entitled to a quarter. In other words, as Clothilde explained with a smile, her parents had just disinherited their younger daughter in favour of the elder, using my son Henri's career as the excuse.

Clothilde laid her hand flat on your desk, offering it to me to take hold of, so that I could clasp it firmly and let her share some of that tenderness which we had stolen from her. That was all that mattered. 'Vanity of vanities, all this property, all this scheming . . .' she murmured, without finishing her sentence. The wall-clock in your study chimed eleven. The sun was shining on the façade of Saint-Pardom. 'As this is such a big house, Roland, you ought to show me round it, help me to love it and explain it perhaps a little.'

Will you understand, Joseph, if I tell you that for one moment I had the impression that it was you who were talking to me? Clothilde withdrew her hand from my grasp and sitting back in your chair again, clasping the armrests with the palm of her hands, a favourite position of yours, she started to explain, half-amused, half-regretful, what she referred to as 'Sabine's calculations'. All her phrases started with the words 'according to Sabine's calculations . . .' But never once in her voice and still less in her admissions was there a trace of resentment. Sabine was and always had been the prettier of the two. The livelier one and the more unyielding too in playing all the little games of life. And Clothilde seemed to find some amusement in recounting all those childhood memories which bore witness to the rejecting of one sister in favour of the other, to a preference for the elder at the expense of the younger, to all the ingenuity Sabine had displayed since the age when she played with dolls in concentrating upon herself all the hopes of her parents, who from being small tradesfolk had become the proprietors of the Bazaar and still dreamed of greater things to come.

There was no sarcasm in Clothilde either. And no hope of anything in return for revealing this. She knew that in exchange I would tell her nothing of how the two of us had managed to be and to remain together, for neither she nor Sabine had been able to impinge in any true sense on our union.

It is time I reminded you once again of my desire to reach a clearer

definition of ourselves, for these first texts I have copied out in no
sense convey the way we constantly surprised one another every
morning, every evening, every night of our lives. No matter
whether it's the story of Sandro who died drowning under a
leaden sky, or 'El Col' implanting his dagger, of a rainbow whose
gates we are still opening now, or of a donkey disembowelled
before our very eyes, this is all peripheral to what we were. In the
passages I shall choose henceforth, I shall attempt to reconstitute
the core of our relationship, its body and its soul, our 'creation' if
you like, or our continuous struggle.

By letting me take over your study, by asking me to come back as
often as I like, by inviting me to sort out and classify things or
throw them away where necessary, Clothilde is helping me to
keep you alive and thus reveals a need in herself as urgent as my
own.

Then Clothilde rose quickly to her feet, as if afraid she might start
crying, in dread of those smarting tears which have so little to do
with sorrow. She turned towards the library shelves, selected a
book and flicked through the pages, careful not to dislodge the
markers or your notes. She half-whispered: 'All those journeys
you made together, one day I shall just ask you to tell me about
them. But I suppose it will always seem too soon to do that. It's
not, my dear Roland, that I want to know all about you both, just
that I'd like to find out perhaps, before I'm too old, who he was,
the man I lived with, who gave me children who in turn . . .'

The sentence hung in mid-air. She turned to face me, drying her
eyes, and elaborated: 'Everything has passed me by! I should have
realized it years ago, as soon as I got palmed off with Sabine's
cast-off toys, all those dolls she'd slashed with her scissors as she
cut off their clothes to make more beautiful dresses for them to
wear!'

I stood up. I took Clothilde in my arms and kissed her on the
brow. She said: 'Thank you.' She slipped away to move around by

herself and inspect all the books, pictures and antiques that you gathered into this den where we have so often worked at the same table, face to face, with our knees interlocked, covering each other's bare feet. And smiling as she did the first day we all met and you gave her that military salute. Clothilde looked at me. A clean straight look. 'I'll leave you in here. Don't go. Stay...' And she disappeared, closing the door as softly as one does the first day of a love affair, so as not to wake one's lover up. Those tender newlyweds at Montestruc! How one thing cuts across another. And they all slice through me. I could almost lick the blood from my hands like the handsome Antoine. If we care to think of it, we are all assassins with blood on our hands.

Our love, Joseph, is unique in one thing: that we have lived it without dreaming that there could ever be anything better. We were proprietorial all right, but only about ourselves. Besotted.

I stayed in your study quite late, until the evening. I left Saint-Pardom by the kitchen-garden gate. Clothilde had left it open, no doubt as a mark of complicity. Sabine was waiting for me in front of her geraniums. Clothilde, sitting next to her, was drinking a cup of tea. Clothilde was wearing a light-coloured dress, whereas the dark-clad Sabine was still signalling her mourning. Sabine advised me that we were dining at her parents' and that I had only one hour to get ready. I went up to my study and picked up this notebook. So here quickly is my message for today. And one picture. Clothilde with her hair drawn back and knotted in a bun, her face smooth and almost radiant, welcoming me to Saint-Pardom, to a reunion in our home. It is her home now, and her open happy smile tells me that her mourning is as luminous as a cotton frock in springtime. Till tomorrow.

# *Eighth day*

I count the days that separate me from the day you died. It's my way to count backwards. So that I can stay on my feet.

Curious folk these Bérards, our parents-in-law, whom we have never addressed by any names but Monsieur and Madame, unable as we were to subscribe to the rituals of family affection. I shall go one better in this account of their dinner party and stick to calling them Old Man Bérard and Old Mother Bérard, which were the names we gave them *entre nous*. By now they are quite an old couple. Is it unfair of me to say that the sight of their daughter Clothilde in a light-coloured dress barely one week after your funeral suddenly added years to them? All at once they were a hundred, and when they asked us to sit down at the table they looked as if they'd been stuffed or turned to stone. They blamed me for arriving 'so very late' and causing 'problems with the cook', and prattled on nervously about 'our *soufflé* that probably couldn't wait'. Old Mother Bérard asked me teasingly: 'But how do you spend so much time in that study of yours? What are you counting?'

Sabine never stopped talking. Notably about your family vault which according to her needed repairs to the roof. As though this should have stirred her sister or captured my attention. Then it was Henri's turn. He hadn't written since he got back to Paris, but he must be suffering from the hot weather, poor boy, at such an important moment in his life.

The *soufflé* had waited. It was delicious. Old Mother Bérard seemed satisfied, because she congratulated the cook. But each time the latter retired to the kitchen she was recalled by the jingling of a little silver bell and reminded in a far less agreeable tone of voice that she had forgotten either the salt or the seasonings or still more important the medicaments for Monsieur.

Old Man Bérard, deafer than ever, no doubt incapacitated by the backfiring of his motor-cars, made not the slightest effort to follow what was said round the table. He was happy enough mopping up his plate with his bread. 'It's not done,' cried Old Mother Bérard. 'You know it's not, and yet you persist in doing it.' Unimpressed, Old Man Bérard fixed Clothilde with a prolonged stare and muttered: 'I like your dress, you look prettier that way . . .' This made Sabine cross: 'That's right, Papa, you side with her.' An oddly childish gathering round that table. Two octogenarians and three fifty-year-olds, all bickering. I believe I winked at Clothilde. Clothilde delicately dabbed at her lips and then stretched out her hand for the *soufflé*. 'I think I shall have some more.' 'You wait until you're asked. Joseph, you tell her.' 'Oh no, Madame, not Joseph. My name is Roland.' Confusion. Silence.

And that's that. I had to report that *lapsus linguae*, didn't I? Old Man Bérard missed it completely. Sabine and her mother blushed. Clothilde and I glanced at each other, almost amused. Suddenly we were happy. You were undeniably present.

Then, to create a diversion, Old Mother Bérard took it into her head to talk about the Bazaar and her employees who were all demanding holidays, arguing that *she* had never travelled anywhere and that travel was the prerogative of artists. 'Those trips of yours, Roland . . . what did you learn from them?' 'How nice it was to come home again, Madame.'

On the table was the best dinner service and the finest silver. All sorts of gleaming melodramatic objects of the kind one produces when one wants to lend importance to events that have none at all. Over dessert, Old Mother Bérard gracefully laid her napkin down on the tablecloth, swung her chair slightly round to face us and addressing herself to Clothilde and to me announced that she had something very important to tell us. I think Clothilde broke into a laugh. I say 'I think', because her laughter was so quiet, so self-effacing, that it was begging to pass unnoticed. Clothilde rose from the table, kissed her mother on the forehead, stroked the nape of Sabine's neck, then went up to her father and, with her hands round his shoulders, bent over him and whispered: 'No, really, I don't think that sort of thing's important.' Her father asked her to repeat what she had said and Clothilde laughed and said it again out loud. Her father smiled. She offered him her cheek and he kissed it.

It is odd that none of these notes I've unearthed to provide the framework of my story make any reference at all to these dinners with the Bérard family. Doubtless we left out any hint of satire in expressing the difference between them and us or our indifference to them. Or the futility of the habit common in their circles of calculating everything in terms of money. What I am writing today is an attempt to repair this oversight and pin down a triviality.

So Sabine, now reigning in glory, has waited for you to die before weaving her web and putting her strategy into effect. Through her mother she has obtained everything. In our country fathers are either unmentionable or mad, and the women rule the roost. Clothilde, thwarted as a child, had no choice but to join up with us.

When Sabine and I walked her home to Saint-Pardom, Clothilde was quite cheerful. She made a few simple remarks, like: 'I love this town. This place. Everything here. It gives me all I need.' She glanced at her sister to make sure she had been listening. And when, in front of the gates, Sabine, somewhat embarrassed, felt compelled to ask if she wouldn't rather come back to live at

Copeyne, Clothilde answered mildly: 'But Sabine, you've already sold the house. If Roland isn't happy staying in Paris, he can come to Saint-Pardom. And so can you, if Paris doesn't live up to your expectations . . .' When Sabine mentioned that it wasn't wise to leave the gates open day and night, Clothilde put in: 'It will always be like that now. Open wide. I have nothing to hide.' And she looked at me as if she were asking me to repeat it to you. As if she knew that during this last week I had spent all my mornings, my days and my nights in communication with you. That was it. Some birds wait for hours after their prey is dead before they devour it. And it is the same with all literature. We have destroyed our poems, but the looks we exchanged, our fidelity, our emotions have not yet been consumed – nor the rapacity of others which can do nothing against the resistance of children who swap their pencil-cases or only receive from their elder sisters dolls that have been slashed to pieces.

This true text, this sequence of notes will recreate our own hell, our own truth. Enough beating about the bush. Now for our bodies. May they stretch and sprawl between these sheets of paper in everlasting initiation. The scandal lies only in that crude material, the ink.

# 11 December 1907. From Joseph.
## The Egg

I dreamt that I was eating an egg and that you were inside it. Should I perhaps, in order to intensify the dramatic effect of this note, which in a few minutes I shall slip between the pages of the book you are busy reading as you sit facing me on the far side of my desk, have given a more detailed description of my dream-egg and not revealed so suddenly what I found inside it? I could see myself sitting at one end of the bed on which we were both asleep, draped round each other in a rather threatening way, as though locked in a wrestlers' embrace, with me on my back and you half on top of me, face down, your left hand pressing my right hand down flat on the sheet. The dream: all very present.

Here I am, a voyeur at one end of the bed, with someone (I say someone because in fact I can't see anyone) bringing me a tray in the centre of which sits an egg in an egg-cup. No egg spoon, no knife, no salt, no toast, nothing else to suggest that this might be the start of a breakfast. What should I do? Sitting with the tray on my knees I gaze at the motionless couple asleep. I listen to the noises of the night: the sounds of the house, an unobtrusive creaking, a muffled but distinctive continuo, as though all our furniture and knick-knacks had united in concert to express their amusement at the scene; and the sounds from outside: the whistling of the wind as it twisted and spiralled round the house, a frost-bearing wind, so cosy to listen to when the embers are glowing in the hearth.

That egg fascinates me. Still warm, just right, soft and slightly runny no doubt, exactly how I like them. And the way you prepare them when it's your turn to get the breakfast. But how do I eat it?

Fear prevents me from waking us up to ask for our advice. So there is no alternative. I pick it up between the thumb and forefinger of my left hand, and to remove the crown bite into it. This I do with great caution. Then I place the egg back in the egg-cup and spit out the top of the eggshell, taking care not to swallow the smallest fragment.

With my hands resting on the edge of the tray, I stoop down over the egg as if about to suck it. I notice that it is underdone. Just inside the shell the white is far from firm and at the centre, floating in liquid, the yolk starts swimming round, turning darker and pinker till it's almost the colour of a child's skin: it's you, it's you there inside my egg. Very tiny. Like a miniature you. Like a live foetus, but with your adult features. Quite repulsive. I find this dream so invidious that I order myself to wake up. But there is no response. I no longer obey my own bidding. I can do nothing but stare at you.

And there we are on the bed in front of me, as if petrified by sleep, effigies of flesh and blood with their winding sheets removed. The tray grows heavier on my knees as though it were trying to pin me to my chair, to the parquet. The desire to lean forward increases. But my hands seem glued to the handles of the tray. The silence in the house grows more insistent, like a beating heart, the heart of all things that are inert until dreams breathe life into them. Yes, everything begins to shake. And that black biting December wind whirls round every corner of Saint-Pardom, as though it intended to uproot our house, cellars and all, like a gigantic tooth.

Oh what a wonderful dream! The more unlikely a dream is, the more tempted one is to say it was wonderful.

You in an egg? In my egg? One that has been boiled especially for me and brought to my bedroom as a great treat?

This could all become quite grotesque. While I am composing this note, you pretend not to notice that I am writing it, as you know it is destined for you. It's all a game. But this is a message you won't tear up. You'll say: 'No, I want to keep this another day.' And I'm very much afraid that, knowing you, that day will last forever. So read what comes next and then read it again and again.

Unable to shake off my dream by waking, and finding no other means of escaping the situation, I decided to analyse what is happening to me. Oh yes, you can still analyse your dream while you're dreaming. And sometimes our reawakening will instantly eclipse the fragile understanding at the moment it was being grasped and embraced, wiping the magic slate clean to leave us desolate, with a memory we cannot formulate of something we have lost forever, like an unfulfilled desire.

But this time, while dreaming and interpreting my dream – that feeling of petrifaction facing our bed, the tray and the egg – I shall write down each step in the analysis to be sure to make this the exception that proves the rule of the blackboard being swept clean.

First I tell myself that this egg is our death. The futility of our ejaculations, of all the seed I sow in you and you in me, impartially as we change round, reversing the dominant role in our battling embraces, all this seminal ritual wasted. And isn't this little mannikin you, my friend Roland, here in this liquid, spitting out whatever he has drunk from me, while curiously gestating in the secretions of my body?

Then, rejecting this interpretation as being too far-fetched, I like to imagine that in fact we are both in the one egg, each swallowing the other. And that you'll probably say to me in mockery of my dream: 'I had just the same one, the same time as you.'

90

So then I wanted that egg. I had to swallow you, just as you swallow me. There is something odd, extremely urgent about this present. So I wrench my hands off the tray, leaving a little raw skin sticking to the handles. My hands start bleeding. I have to be quick, and I pick the egg up, suck and swallow. I can feel you go down inside me and immediately grow and grow until you are as big as I am, until you are me!

It was you who woke me up. You were grinning. Gazing at my belly. And then you said: 'Are you sufficient unto yourself now?'

This is one climax I stole from you. But I shall give it back. A brutal message. An exquisite corpse.

# 7 January. From me. Joseph at the piano

You never give any warning. Any time will do whenever you want to take me by surprise. Or am I just imagining that you sit down at the piano for my sake? You always choose a moment when I am not in the drawing-room. Sometimes even, when I am just back from the town, I can hear you from the gates and I am torn between the delightful thought that this is your way of welcoming me, of offering me asylum even, and frank irritation at the idea, which I refuse to accept, that at times you want to play without my being there to listen.

Is this a quarrel? Do such mixed feelings of pleasure and irritation deserve to be dwelt on? Or is it unworthy of two men whose confrontation has led them to share all their thoughts and all their feelings?

A few minutes ago you left the study, saying 'I won't be long.' I knew you were going to play. I heard you making for the bathroom on this floor and then turn off towards the staircase, creep down the stairs, cross the kitchen and pass through the pantry and the dining-room to reach the drawing-room. Rather an odd route, wasn't it? I suppose you will claim that as neither of us is able to fool the other this is an expression of the spontaneity that lies on the behavioural fringe of any sentimental attachment. Perhaps you will make an ironic comment, accusing me again in your favourite cliché of being 'romantal and sentimentic'. Go on, Joseph, I'm listening. You told me you 'wouldn't be long' so that I would stay where I was. So that I shouldn't watch you sit down at the piano, select a piece of music and put on those thick lenses you've been wearing lately, like a pair of magnifying glasses. Ridiculous and rather touching. They hint at mediocrity. Or is it distinction? There comes a point when one lapses so easily into one extreme or the other that one can't tell the difference any more.

And now you are playing the solo part of the *Andante* from Mozart's Concerto No.21. Listening to you, I understand now. You don't want me there, standing behind you and watching. You want me to be somewhere up here, listening attentively, as moved as you are to be picking your way through this or that melody again, preferring as you always do to sight-read rather than work at interpretation.

You told me this music had character and temper. And I quote you: 'The temper of the seasons and the character of a landscape.' But there is nothing narrative about Mozart. His work is too close to Nature. And Nature never narrates. It is content to be what it is. It was Mankind that started telling stories.

And now in January the music sounds different from last summer, or even the one before that, when the french windows of the drawing-room stood open, letting overpowering whiffs of damp earth float to our heads, and when the song of the nightingale chimed with the notes of a sonata. Yes, it all sounds so idyllic, but I admit that and you welcome it. And I know this sort of thing only lasts for a while. I can feel the passing of the years. What you are playing now pains me profoundly. Oh, what power they have to alter us, those plaintive *andantes* proclaiming life so urgently. The whole house echoes with them. So it is not often that I have seen you playing the piano. And that fills me with reproach, jealousy almost. But jealousy is not the fear of losing, but the dread of sharing.

Sometimes, in this study, I get up while you are playing and beat my fists against the walls – always that hull, always Sandro –

93

thumping against you in a desperate effort to force my way out, or in, to lose my whole self, to find a permanent home for myself in you. So our separate bodies, two unique domains of folds and hollows, will always be there, keeping us apart, tempting us to clothe ourselves in one another.

Whether the piece of music you play is exactly what I am expecting, or whether you take me by surprise, anticipating an unexpressed desire, how can it help but disarm me further in my quest for you? And when you come back, your emotions stirred, I feel it is the same for you. Strange harmony.

The more your sight-reading stumbles, the more appealing is the poignancy of the notes and the more pervasively the melodic harmonies invade our space and penetrate every corner of this, our house. Then caressing waves of sound arrive, somewhat shyly but with badgering tenderness, until all the air here trembles and vibrates expectantly. Like a gnawing hunger pleading to bring us together.

At other times too, in the autumn or the spring, when I am lingering in the gardens and you have pretended to go in and fetch your tobacco or a cooling drink and suddenly I hear you playing, then I can watch Saint-Pardom quiver as it bursts into song. And you are the magician who casts this spell over space, with the tips of your fingers. Listening intoxicates me. It's like a fine piece of oratory our walls take pleasure in. The sky itself, the elm and the evergreen oaks in the park seem to join together in concert. I could even say, with some exaggeration, that it has all been orchestrated. But I know, when you read such a far-fetched description, that you will either tone it down or accept it in all modesty. Has it become so inadmissible to try to enjoy our lives and make the most of our best moments in time?

And when you touch me afterwards, slipping your hand through the half-open collar of my shirt, I bite my lips or clench my teeth so as not to start shaking. You tease me and ask if I'm cold:

'You've got gooseflesh!' And I move away from you and tell you to leave me alone. Jealous! At the piano you make love to the house and force me to be there while you do it. A great celebration for all of us, which I'd rather have all for myself. I reveal a weakness in what I've just written. But I don't give a damn. That's the way it is. This evening I'll pounce on you. And as you sit smiling at the piano, I tell myself that's what you're waiting for.

# 9 September 1908. From Joseph.
## Tityre the Cat

He flings the pantry door open without knocking. He bursts in. What if we are there? It's quite natural! It's nine-year-old Martial. We haven't seen him for four years, but in his mind we've only been waiting for him. He sets a large basket down on the table and removes the handkerchief he had tied round his head. Midday. He looks us straight in the eyes as though it were only yesterday we last saw each other and says: 'Good morning, Joseph. Good morning, Roland,' just like old friends. 'I've brought you a cat. He's my favourite. "El Col's" men want to eat him.'

I believe you smiled, Roland, before I did. Up to a point you have also trained me not to lose my temper: a profound yet pointless impulse to testiness has been checked and overlaid by the regular rhythm and habits of the well-ordered days we have spent together. I shall think of Martial's entrance as a sudden apparition. He opens the door! Here he is! It's him! We were expecting him! And that amuses you, Roland? Right, I accept it! I'm listening! Martial says: 'I'm thirsty.' You hand him a glass of water. Martial asks me if I'm angry. You answer for me: 'He's always like this!'

Then Martial stands on tiptoe and leaning on the big kitchen table slowly slides out the reed that holds the lid down and opens his basket. And the cat pops out of its prison like a jack-in-the-box. A fat tom-cat with a sleek black coat, in white boots with a rather bright pink nose. The sort of cat you'd find anywhere. 'And he's in good condition,' affirms Martial as he pulls back his cheeks, in a tone that he has doubtless heard his father use at the fair when selling a beast. Then silence. An anxious Martial asks us repeatedly whether we intend to keep his cat. And you, Roland, amused, answer vaguely with a string of 'perhaps', 'we'll see', 'if you're a good boy'. To the last remark Martial reacts with an, 'All right, I'll take him back.' It was my turn to intervene. 'We'll keep him, Martial, nobody's going to eat him.'

The cat stretches, arches his back, then sits and conscientiously licks first one paw then the other, little white paws with pads the same pink colour as his nose, as though he wished to be at his best to inspect his adoptive home. Many tales are invented about animals, but are they pure invention? 'Was it your father who told you to come?' 'No.' 'You told him you were coming?' 'No.' 'And did you walk from La Sarriete?' 'No.' 'How did you come then?' 'Roundabout way!' The expression on Martial's face darkens. I am asking too many questions. The cat jumps on the table. Martial puts his glass away in the sink, looks at Roland, then smiles at me: 'He wants to look round. So do I . . .'

We follow the cat, which is inspecting every nook and cranny of the pantry. 'And what's his name?' 'Cat!' 'Couldn't you think of anything else?' 'All my cats are called Cat. Cat Number 1, Number 2, Number 3.' 'And what's the number of this one?' 'He hasn't got one. He's just Cat. He's the best one.' 'Why?' 'He keeps to himself. He's only nice if you don't ask him to be nice.' 'Like you?' Martial shrugs his shoulders.

The cat is our guide. The dining-room does not seem to interest him much. He walks straight into the drawing-room, rubbing against the armchairs, sniffing the cushions, testing out his claws on a rug. I am about to stop him but Roland prevents me. 'Oh, no! This is his home now!' Martial is delighted. The cat leaps on the piano-stool, which spins round, creaking a little. Terrified, the cat dives off and disappears into the hall. The stool tips over and Martial sets it straight. He starts picking out notes with one finger. Every note amuses him. He looks at us in astonishment,

97

thrilled. 'You won't tell my father, will you?' You tell him we won't, but I don't answer. Are *we* abducting *him*, or is it vice versa?

The cat climbs to the first floor. We follow. Martial calls out to him: 'Cat! Cat! You're at home now, that's what they said.' The cat halts in front of the attic door. 'You'll have to keep that door open. Cat likes mice!' Martial opens the door. The tom-cat dashes in and disappears. 'I'm still thirsty. Can we go down again?'

Martial is lunching with us. He holds his knife and fork firmly in his fists. You look at me bashfully. I lower my eyes. We have a child at our table. We have a child. And that, on the face of it, is both heartening and disquieting. Every smile from Martial becomes almost threatening. Is he making fun of us? What does he know about us? What instinct is drawing him to us? Thinking all this, I know that you are thinking the same at the very same time. We have both turned thirty and here we are living a cloistered life, selfishly taking pleasure in each other's company, in vital need of each other's confidences, reading, making music, fortifying and loving one another. And now this child arrives, shattering us. He is bringing more than a cat. He is bringing himself. I know he'll come back. He is watching you. Copying you already. He grips his knife just as you do yours. We lunch in silence. When Martial has finished, he puts his plate in the sink. Then he clears yours and mine away. No doubt that is what he does at home. But now he is doing it in our house too and there is something servile about it. You make a sign to me not to move.

'It's time for you to go home, Martial.' 'They can wait.' 'All right, we'll come with you.'

The cat reappears, stroking the wall, with his tail up, his whiskers alert and his ears pricked back a little. 'He's happy,' Martial murmurs, 'that's his way of telling us. What are you going to call him?' You turn to me and smile: 'We'll call him Tityre.' Martial gazes in astonishment. 'It's the name of a shepherd. Tityre . . . say

98

it, Tityre!' Martial picks the cat up in his arms and says: 'They want to call you Tityre, do you like it?'

On the road to La Sarriete, Martial knots his handkerchief round his head again. 'The Spaniards taught me to tie it like this.' Martial is carrying his sandals in the empty basket, walking barefoot. The dust is scorching. It is three o'clock in the afternoon. 'You're not going to school yet?' 'Don't want to!' 'But . . .' 'I won't, Joseph! Roland, I won't!' He looks animatedly from one to the other. 'But I want to learn how to write.' 'How then?' 'In your house! I'll come and see Tityre.'

Then I saw you take Martial's hand. We would arrange it all with Robert. Thus everything was oddly settled. A child was about to slip between us. And I remembered the way you had held little Elie against you at Montestruc that evening of the Moonfishers. And I told myself that in separating us this child would be just as likely to draw us together. Perhaps we have reached the age, Roland, when everything tends to crystallize and petrify into rock-hard stone.

So when Martial, with his basket, pushed that door open without knocking, he came to impose upon us a new order, a different discipline, which will perhaps also become a kind of passion. A fresh aspect of ourselves.

Robert did not appear surprised. 'I thought he was out in the fields. He's often away for whole days.' Once again we drank his bitter liqueur. Martial stood in one corner of the room, arms folded like a grown-up. He was listening. His father looked at us and said: 'I'd rather know he was with you, Monsieur Joseph, than God knows where! And if Monsieur Roland manages to teach him to read and write, I shall be very proud of you both. But never of course of him!' He motioned his son to approach and kissed him on the brow, as if to remove the reproach.

When we regained Saint-Pardom, Tityre was waiting for us. A

whole family had just entered our lives. And I can see you are happy, Roland, as though the whole scheme had been engineered in advance.

A child turns up, carrying a basket with a cat inside. There we were and here they are! What mysteries the future holds! A new centre for our eccentricity to focus on. A young body to satisfy our wishes, to watch as he grows, with Tityre as our accomplice!

# 11 September 1908.
## From me: bursts of laughter

I have just bought the *Dépêche*, the last two issues of
*L'Illustration* and a whole stock of exercise-books, pencils, a
pencil-sharpener, blotting-paper and above all a pencil-case for
our scholar. At the cash-till of her Bazaar, Madame Bérard
remarks with amusement, just as I am paying the bill, that I have
no basket to carry my purchases in. She tells one of her girls to
make one parcel of everything. She only needs to turn her head to
one side for her voice to change and take on a rather sharp, almost
acid tone in order to imply that a new piece of string and the best
wrapping-paper are not required. Then she turns back to me,
smiles and asks after my health. I wonder why? And my plans for
the future? This really does take me by surprise. Then she goes on
to complain that life is so complicated, there's no time to see
anyone, even when your neighbours live quite near. There was
sarcasm in that 'even when', with a touch of frustration. 'Yet we
promised we would see more of each other. How long ago was
that now?' A smile passes over my face and she takes it to be a
polite one, though in fact it was addressed to myself and to us,
Joseph, at the thought of all those years we have devoured in our
greed for one another, like two gluttons who never took the time
to wipe their lips. That was the image that provoked my smile.
Then Madame Bérard starts talking about her daughters, who, as
she says, 'are doing very well at the Carmelite school, especially
Sabine who . . .' But I can judge from the woman's urgency that
she is telling me everything but the one basic fact that matters.
Ordinary but dramatic. She is hiding something. Several times she
asks with a dark anxious look how *you* are, only to return with a

101

smile to reminiscences of that wedding and then stumble back to you. Again and again, she won't leave it alone and that annoys me. When the parcel is wrapped, I give the girl a sou, and Madame Bérard gets cross. She tells her to hand the coin back. I return a categorical 'No' and escape with the packet under my arm, refusing to admit to myself that any conversation outside our own home not limited to the barest platitudes is unacceptable.

At the Lion d'Or café I drink a shandy as usual. But I am greeted distantly. People pretend not to see me. What makes this morning so different from the others? What are we suddenly accused of? Aren't we just the two old bachelors in town, neither seen nor heard and hardly known at all? Is it common knowledge already that Martial visits us every day and that we are giving him lessons?

I decide to take a roundabout way home. Again I am greeted distantly or else not greeted at all. At the bottom of the rue des Cordeliers I meet Surrelac, who looks away as if I had just caught him red-handed in the act of adultery. When I reached the Boulevard de Gesles, I understood.

There was a gathering in front of the steps to the Rigand House. I looked up at the window of your father's bedroom on the first floor, shutters closed. Signs and sidelong glances convey to me that I had better not join the group outside. I content myself with slowing my pace, to give me time to reflect. So you will never have seen your father. He will never have spoken to you. We had forgotten him too.

And for the first time I return to Saint-Pardom slowly, without desire, wondering how I am to break the news of the death of a man who was never dear to you. In situations like this it is so easy to be condescending, to invent all manner of pointless refinements or brutal subterfuges. Or even craven evasions, as when one opts for silence, leaving someone else to make the clumsy announcement or letting rumour creep up and deliver the blow, the bad news the victim has no inclination to hear.

All of a sudden that old father of yours was going to be extremely important. He would be going to the cemetery, the other town next to the town, to find another resting-place of stone, without steps this time, where he would once again be separated from your mother! The paths there, aren't they rather like boulevards? As I walk I feel terribly remote from those two towns, almost angry coming back to you with only four words to say: 'Your father is dead.'

That's all. And it's a heavy burden. And here I am, hesitating, imagining different ways of getting to the point, by dropping this or that hint to lead you up to the news, to bring you to say it without having to say it myself. Or else not to go home at all. To wait until, puzzled by my continued absence, you come in search of me and discover for yourself, through friends who change pavements, evasive glances or faltering shopkeepers, that a drama involving you has just unfolded. A drama for them. But not for us. The death of a father is only a rope that snaps. It almost amuses me to think of you in your turn sending a sheaf of red roses with a broad ribbon reading: 'To my beloved father.'

I draw near to Saint-Pardom. Here I am at the gate. None of the usual music. And with all its shutters closed to keep cool inside, our house seems to be dreading my return. Outside the drawing-room the buzzing of the bees in the wistaria and the clematis is like a barrier to break through. And there you are, sitting at the piano, not playing. You turn to face me. I stand still and, leaning back against the frame of the french window, I stare at you for a while and end by saying, in a voice too clear to be mine but in the innocuous tone of the townsfolk: 'Your father is dead, Joseph.'

Then you start laughing. A short laugh, dry and nervous. 'Good!' you say and, pressing your hands hard down on your knees to stand up, you come to me. You take the parcel into the dining-room and untie it on the table. I join you there. 'It's a lovely pencil-case.' That is all you said.

Whereupon Martial arrives for his first lesson. You lead him straight into your study. I remain alone in the drawing-room with Tityre. Keeping one eye on the gate for the petty messenger who is bound to come from town to break the news officially, in the belief that it will upset us and make us suffer. So Tityre and I were on guard, doing our duty: watch-dog and watch-cat!

Then from the belfry of the Cathedral of Saint-Pierre comes the heavy tolling of the knell. Interminably. For notabilities it is always a lengthy process. And to me this knell is a kind of tit-for-tat. The bell that condemned my father is now condemning yours. An exchange of fathers, or the two of them fused together. How old we will be one day! Only now do I understand your laughter. All this pathetic ritual. What are you thinking up there, showing Martial how to grip a penholder and guiding his wrist while you teach him how to write his '*a*'s, then his '*b*'s and his '*c*'s . . .

The bell ceased tolling. Suddenly time hangs heavy in the echoing house. Tityre is sitting in an armchair, staring at me. I imagine he too has understood. And I send him a smile. Like a laugh!

At midday Martial comes tumbling downstairs, walks up to me and says: 'It's easy, I know as far as H! And I'm Hungry, very Hungry. I've never been so Hungry before.'

At table Martial asks: 'Is it for the dead, they toll the bell?' 'No, Martial, for the living.' And the little lad bursts out laughing too, without quite knowing why.

# 29 September 1908. From Joseph.
## Our banquet of bodies

Yours is the body of days and of seasons. Your body is never the same. Sometimes, watching you, I feel you don't belong to yourself. Your skin never catches the light or the shade in the same way twice. Your body huddled up, curled round itself, your body as it was ready to leave your mother's womb: after each sleep you are born again, delivered afresh before my eyes. Or your body face down, flat out on the sheet, your legs and arms in a V, as if fallen from Heaven: every awakening presents me with the sight of you after this fall. At times, when you hold me in your arms, when I crush myself against you, everything starts spinning. No weight to hamper us. Whirling through space.

Yours is the body of days and of seasons. Your body is never the same. Your skin redolent of our rambles. It takes the scent of the wind or the grass. It retains the smell of loose earth and the perfume of the hawthorn. Your skin has an odour that almost scratches. I immerse in its pungency and it reminds me of strong spirits. Every fold in your body exudes its own particular perfume. Each one of your pores seems like a mouth from which I inhale everything you have absorbed, the rain and the light, the sun and the night. Every scent, every odour, every perfume is a discovery for me. You are the whole of nature compressed into one body, as if it had been seized in one fist.

Yours is the body of days and of seasons. Your body is never the same. And for us the daytime is a time for watching. I observe you, fully dressed, as you move, walk, read or work, or busy yourself with this or that household task. I track you down. I lie in wait. I imagine you, beneath your clothes, gathering all sorts of odours for me. What you inhale and hold fast by day, I breathe in at night. And sometimes when I see you smiling, keeping me at arm's length during an embrace to catch a moment's breath, I know that you are happy to be giving me this constant changing exhalation of yourself. Nothing about you ever becomes familiar to me. I do not recognize you. I observe you all through the day, knowing from habit that we shall only be united at night, and wonder what is the nature of the body I shall find, what body that particular day will offer. And so time passes from day to day. And you astound me with the reserves of life you store up beneath your clothing.

Yours is the body of days and of seasons. Your body is never the same. Terrefort loves Raillac. And Raillac lives for him and lives in him. And Terrefort is inspired by him. Shall we always be able to reanimate each other? Let this be our secret: our abandonment. You shall only read this text, Roland, if you survive me; it says and celebrates so much! But if poetry there is, who will accept it? Above all, it must not be spoken of. The only possible influence it can have is by getting woven into the torments and aspirations of each one of us in the most sequestered of solitudes. And if you die before me, at least I will have expressed what I have written here in as many looks and glances when, impatient with our embraces, we sometimes draw apart to contemplate each other. At such moments desire of a different kind rises within me. So I bend over your hips to caress an indentation in your skin made by a belt that was pulled too tight, or to kiss the arch of one foot, that massive hump where all the bones converge and fan out to ensure you a firm stance. Nothing about you is ordinary. Yes, I caress your feet. I have even been known to lick them or to suck at one of your toes. And in that case I imagine myself as an acrobat, holding you upright over my head, as though you had sprung straight out of your toe. Brandishing the whole of you, sprung straight from my mouth like a gigantic phallus, and there is nothing taller than we are. Then you lean over me, seize hold of my head and tell me to stop. It tickles. I am amazed to find no end to my explorations.

Yours is the body of days and of seasons. Your body is never the same. And there behind your knees, what have I found? Hollows again, this time full of salt with a taste like blood. Occasionally too, between my teeth, I chew on one of your hairs. Beautiful, every part of you. How I long to find a way to express all this as intensely true as are those shared silences, those impulsive clashes, those embraces that sharpen the desires through which we are reborn again and again. Only those who refuse to admit that they are what they are experience lassitude. Nothing is dirty save for those who do not know how to love, how two people should love, so that each sees the other as he really is, ever-changing at the behest of time. The body is not all. But everything comes to pass through the body, marked pages of the mind.

Yes, Roland, I seek these marks in you. You are time passing, absorbing and transforming. And when on occasion I moisten the nape of your neck and follow the way down to the small of your back to nestle below that and burrow away and lap the crater with my darting tongue, it is partly enjoyment of a childish game, like riding down a slide or a toboggan, partly in response to the most urgent of adult imperatives, a compulsion to gain entry. Clean and honest. Everything about the human animal is clean and honest.

And there I am engrossed, kissing that curious mouth. A voyeur, watching myself and watching you as well. A whole band of rapists prying at the gateway of your body. You arch up a bit and pull away, and then I feel rising with me, close as I am and almost panting for breath, a furious urge to bite into you or die. I lift myself up, grope for the axis of your body, find the dominant position, dive and slip into you. Then everything envelops and conceals us. The night is fleece-like and I harden. You grip the sheets. I nibble the nape of your neck, get lost in your hair and rediscover the perfume of the day's winds, the late-afternoon sun, a wisp of straw or a wilting petal. As I enter you, you spring up whole out of me. And if I circle you with my hands, it is to grasp your fullness as I would my own. You are my double. I insert myself in successive thrusts and we explode together. Enjoy the same climax.

And if it is your turn now, to throw me off wildly and pin me to the sheets, like tipping a paving-stone over on its back, it is to discover in the dark night of our bodies the odour of streaming sweat, seeping from both of us in lava-like streaks, and the exasperating aroma that lingers close to the skin inviting regret and lending great poignancy to the dying fall of pleasure. Then you give me what you might call a grooming. You wipe me down with your hands and cheeks, you grasp my flesh and knead it. Then you force me up and we kneel face to face with our hands on our thighs, inspecting one another, conscious once more of the silent house. We can hear Tityre chasing the mice in the attic, and the belfry of the Cathedral of Saint-Pierre proclaiming the lateness of the hour. A dog barks in the distance. A cedar creaks under the impact of the wind. You tell me you are thirsty. And off we go together to stand with our heads tipped back, drinking the water that splatters into the bath. The cold water of the night. And at once it was as if we were swallowng the sky and all its breezes, drinking from the bowl of the horizon.

Roland! Yours is the body of days and of seasons! I gravitate around you. You cast me into space only to pull me back again. Do not let me go, whatever you do, not for one single day. Or I shall fall and fall forever. Time weaves its threads and weaves us into its texture. We wear ourselves out, file and plane each other down. Nothing will be left of us but our ageing bodies. And one day something will snap in one of us. But at this instant, in this series of instants, our descent is a rising fall. It uplifts us, though our whole education taught us to smother and eradicate our feelings. You look at me? Already I am in your eyes. You hold out your hands? Already I am rolling in the furrows of your palms. You take off your clothes? At the sight of your dark phallus, its heavy sack and its bushy fleece, already I am playing truant.

Losing myself in that virgin forest. Saluting my totem pole. Mine is the song that was sung by the shepherds of yesteryear, before lawyers had had the time to do their worst. Before they had claimed the whole of nature as their property. When we were still part of nature. And what name did you choose for this cat? Tityre! That choice alone implies complicity. Here on the outskirts of this town, our ancestral home, our birthplace, we are living a life our century will never know again. Are we perhaps the last survivors of a primitive tribe? Where are the rest, those others we shall never meet again? Ah! If only they knew that we are alive as well. Our great banquet of bodies in restorative. It spells salvation.

Each day that passes gives a sign that our pleasures will be unending. I consume your body, but never have enough of it. I breathe it in and sound its depths, just as you do mine. We shall go on devouring each other and by some magic grace we may learn how to grow old together, who knows? Or will our wild infatuation be limited in time? Now the world has assigned a cat and a child to keep a close eye on us. Or did we ourselves summon them? Here they are anyway. Our movements were never stronger, more precise, more probing and deliberate than when *they* are present. In our confrontations there can never be an ultimate limit. Now I devour every part of you. A body is not governed by codes and modes. A body is its own moral arbiter. The more we press on in our exploration, the more there is left to explore. There lies the mystery, the one God, woven out of time, threaded with loving glances, the stir of passion, the pricking of desire, the taming of our most violent instincts. When we are skeletons, our bones will still be stretching out to one another, dust and ashes, earth of the earth, we shall still seek to be reunited, and that is the way we shall perpetuate ourselves.

And if, as I emerge from you, I am smeared with dirt, I am no longer troubled by disgust. At once I accept this trace of you. This too is part of our banquet of bodies. And I wipe myself, as others dab their lips at a high-class dinner-party. A similar gesture. A similar stain. Similar mouths. There is plenty of mud at certain bends of the Verse or the Gesles, dirty water in certain wells, dead birds rotting in the sun, people who blow their noses and love to scrutinize their snot. Why is it allowed, such vulgarity from them, when this ritual gesture of our love is unacceptable? I want to learn from these words how to reach profounder depths in you. Let them guide me just as I guide little Martial's hand when I teach him how to write. Or as you point out a word with your fingertip when you're teaching him how to read.

The more messages I read from you, the more I feel that I have written them myself. And the more I write, the more I feel it is you, invested in me, making these remarks. Are we so liberated, so integrated, that our embraces, abolishing distance, are perpetuated in thought? Every line I write is like another step down your spine. Every full stop a place to nestle and to burrow. To tap and enter. The warmth of you. I am intoxicated, drunk with you, with clenched fists always brutally ready for you. A lifetime of sharp expectancy, on the *qui vive*! And every evening, within sight and hearing of our sarcastic town, we batter at the gates of each other's bodies and we two alone make love in the whole world.

Yours is the body of days and of seasons. You swell in my mouth. And I drink you down. Oh, you will never be the same Roland twice.

# 13 November 1908. From Joseph.
## Caverns

Every time I place my lips on yours you half open them and I find that taste of you again which quenches every thirst. We are mostly made of water, you know, though not very much of it, our tissues all mucus and saliva, seeping or spurting secretions, rivers going nowhere which at last in the valley between us can furrow out their beds. Our poetry never speaks of what unites us. A text that is too explicit disunites. Yet at times, in the poems you used to show me, the ones we threw away with amusement or disappointment, unable to accept the fact that our poetry was 'us', I would pick out a few passages that invited an exchange, a confession, a challenge to a duel. Inscribed in my memory are two lines written in the train which brought you back to Cazauban and would deliver you to me that day, that great day, when we found each other again: 'The finest form of suicide is to know you're still alive.' Or set out like verse:

> The finest form of suicide
> Is to know you're still alive.

Are we not killing ourselves, Roland, for the pleasure of living? A meaningless question, when one thinks of the gravity of all sexual congress, of our plunging flesh and that struggle for death which is ours, because like our rivers whatever we generate must remain abortive! Yes, we are a perfect example of waste, as useless as a work of art. All those things in our relationship which are banished or effaced are proof of the vanity of any text of ours that claims to express it all.

111

I can't wait to go travelling with you again. Needless long journeys we shall take, for no distance can be too great to bring us more closely together, after the long road we have travelled already to meet and take refuge in the caverns of each other's mouths.

Another of your adolescent poems: 'As the sun was going in the fountain flowing I seemed to see glowing a pool of our blood.' Or set out like verse:

> As the sun was going
> In the fountain flowing
> I seemed to see glowing
> A pool of our blood.

I know, a bit too song-like. Melodious verse is always suspect. Neither of us is a genius, but that's something to be proud of. The fountain overdoes it. Too pretty. And yet it reminds me of the time our mouths first met, of our first kisses, before we realized how many deep springs would be tapped, to gush forth all our zest for life.

And that drama you wrote when you were fifteen, with a scene between Narcissus and a Judge. Narcissus said: 'I wish to learn, but I do not wish to know. Knowing means giving.'

Or again: 'The furies in your fingers are legion. I dare not budge. The enemy has gone to ground.' Or set out like verse:

> The furies in your fingers are legion.
> I dare not budge.
> The enemy has gone to ground.

It is most unfair of me, selecting a few fragments from the whole, but our masterwork is the whole. That is where we leave our true mark. So I shall hide these lines from you too. Perhaps one day you will glimpse in some of these words the care and despair I have put into the cherished hope, the only one that matters maybe, that we have altered each other without altering anything else. Why should we have conformed to the mandates of modern fashion and joined a movement? Why such urgent need for reform? According to the papers there's a fine rumpus going on in Paris. We need an upheaval? The upheaval of our bodies is enough for us!

And when we are separated by the light of day, we scrutinize each other. We have to pass the time, get through that interminable desert, so as to reach out for each other in the evening and seek shelter in the caverns in our bodies.

I love your gleaming teeth, your sharp canines, the inside of your lips. I could draw up an inventory, an anatomy of our kisses, so many of them, day after day as the years go by, a lingering prologue we tend to prolong, an overture to all that follows.

The sheets on our bed receive the substance we spill when we fail irresponsibly at times to control the passions that convulse us and make us sob with delight. How much longer can we continue unscathed to surprise each other like this? Obstinate, we shall go on until our skin splits like a paper bag and our bones snap like matchsticks. For every blow you offer I return as good as I get. And when at times *I* strike *you*, you laugh. A laugh that echoes through the house, startling Tityre away.

You have gone into town and I am waiting. This house too is a mouth, with its teeth and its jaws, and it will close around you when you return. And we brush against its walls, tongues that dart out at us to lick us. All this will never end. This will last forever.

And when I hold your sex, it is like a tree that grows or a post I am attached to. Choking or assaulting me. The only long journeys that matter are around that tree. Any others we might make, in memory of Sandro or of those that are still to come, will lead us back to turn around that tree. If not perhaps round mine. You grab hold of me, plunge and plant yourself, you too there inside me. You and I are two couples in one! Nothing is impossible. And the price we pay is death. A little dying every day, to a dirge of moans and groans. Your mouth is a study in speleology. I explore it. And draw up a macabre map of its geography, with its hollows, vaults and crevices, its membranous folds and its alcoholic trails. All part of the same thing.

When was it you wrote, set out like verse?

> The light that escapes through the tiniest chink
> The damage done by the slightest defect
> All rifts are the same whatever their effect.

And here I am quoting you once more, betraying you again, setting down the words, clumsy ones this time, which fail to give a true expression of us. I am waiting for you. To produce our literary masterpiece, to be together. Every day we grow more violent. Since Martial has been here, our embraces are more like fist-fights. Everything in the house will soon be ruined. We have forgotten the orderly way our furniture and knick-knacks were arranged. This child is spreading disorder. Forcing us one against the other, just as Sandro brought us face to face.

Yesterday I bit you. Your blood had an overpowering taste. Nauseating. I wonder if we really have begun to murder each other at last.

In the caverns of our mouths we found each other again, confronted and accepted one another, ready for anything, assassins! I am going downstairs to play the piano, just for you. Come back soon! What a hammering we'll have!

114

# Thirteenth day

The great clock of time has turned back. Clothilde is happy. I have come home, to *our* home. I can hear her downstairs at Saint-Pardom, determined to make no noise. I am aware of her trying not to make the parquet creak as she treads cautiously from room to room, as if in the silence everything will remind us of your presence.

We only visit the other house for meals, never happier than when we pass through the kitchen-garden gate, leaving Sabine to sort out her finances and prepare Copeyne for the visit of an eventual purchaser. As if Henri had passed his exams already, Sabine now sees herself as the mother of a polytechnic student. She queens it over us, and we can't help being amused. She accuses us of not behaving with sufficient gravity so soon after your death. Not a day passes without some scathing remark to her sister about her refusal to wear black.

Occasionally I can hear Clothilde in the garden as well. Raking the gravel, hollowing the earth round the trunks of the saplings, pulling up the weeds and planting flowers in the stone vases on the terrace. Sabine suggested she might move some of the geraniums from Copeyne. Pulling a wry face and shooting me a glance, Clothilde declined with a sniff. At forty-seven Clothilde has become a young girl again. Or for the first time perhaps, for her upbringing never allowed her to be one until now.

And to complete this portrait of her, I must tell you to what extent I too enter into the spirit of this apparently happy little game, conniving with her in all kinds of glances and signs, sharing little secrets. Occupying this house, lending it an air of gaiety, constantly getting it ready for a possible visitor, we are always watching and waiting for you. You are here.

Clothilde has got it into her head that she wants to learn to play the piano. Sometimes she practises hard at her scales. At first I was rather irritated, though I took care not to show it. Then, listening to her day after day, I began to feel happy about it, almost overjoyed. Everything has to be learnt again from scratch. Playing it by ear, or sight-reading! In the evening under the lime tree near the gates she settles down in the cane chair you used to prefer when you wanted to spend a few hours alone, reading and rereading a book on the rudiments of music which she bought at the Bazaar. Her mother apparently remarked: 'I hope you're not going to take up the piano at your age!' I dislike that expression, 'take up the piano'. So does Clothilde. Old Mother Bérard will slump over her cash-till one day and snuff it at the mere thought of handing out change. That was Clothilde's picture of her, and how she laughed when she told me!

From my study I can see Clothilde under the lime tree, beating time to the music. *Si, mi, la, re, sol, do, fa . . . fa, dol, sol, re, la, mi, si*! She has picked it all up in a few days, her flats and her sharps, from the key of A to the key of G. And when I meet her next, as the time for dinner approaches, she will recite to me her lesson for the day. Our complicity touches everything. It would not take much for me to join her at the piano. But Clothilde declares: 'I'll manage by myself. I can do it alone because my Joseph is here.' Yet every time the words 'my Joseph' unthinkingly fall from her lips, she takes me by the arm, presses close to me, lowers her eyes and whispers with a smile: 'I'm sorry, *our* Joseph.'

Sabine is aware of this complicity. We can tell by how tense it makes her, liable for example to upset a glass inadvertently at table when she catches us exchanging a look, almost harsh in her rebukes when we laugh or smile at some trivial remark. She never stops saying: 'Think if Joseph were here!' But you are, aren't you? You watch Clothilde, bending over her at the piano. Correct her posture when she sits on the stool to play. Teach her how one's touch flows out through the arm, springing from the whole body, a technique you had thoroughly mastered. 'Your whole body plays.' I can still hear you saying it now.

And I guess it's the same thing in life as well, the way it was in our life too, throughout our days together, and in the truth to be found in this notebook. I do more than just write or copy things down: my whole body goes with me as I bend over these pages, these words. I lay myself down on this paper, the fresh clean sheets of our sensual delights.

And our top sheet, we would always throw that off with the blankets. Here we shall be as naked as before or as we shall be again, for the magic of words projects us forward in time, into all that unknown time to come on which we shall sail in our paper boat, beating our fists against the upturned hull.

If today I enjoy noting down all those touching, almost exquisite moments I shared with Clothilde, it is simply to throw into sharper relief all those texts I have copied out before. All this tenderness is far removed from the violence provoked by Martial's entrance into our lives. Accidentally, we had produced a child. He was ours all right, this wild boy who picked up so quickly everything we taught him, as though there were some urgent need in him to join us at the most poignant and intimate heart of our relationship. Our little Martial very soon made a place for himself! Too soon perhaps. But it was he, no one else, who crept between us. Who was it did all the right things? Who conquered us with his eyes? Who persuaded us with his smiles? Who was it who entered without knocking? And did we not know, long before all this developed, that it would only last for a while, when our love had already endured for so long and when, as we looked at each other, we could tell how much older we felt by now?

117

Martial emerged between us like an image of ourselves as children, eager, perfectible, curious about everything. In his one self he combined the two of us, linked in an embrace and leaping into the Verse. Remember how we wanted to die together? But we did die together! We used each other up, wore each other out, devoured, hit and boxed each other, and together we arched our backs and stabbed at one another! But the fatal blow was never delivered. Our climaxes cheated us of death. Until the day when, shortly after luncheon, Martial said abruptly: 'It's hot, why don't we go and sleep upstairs?'

He was eleven. June 1909. I can find nothing written for that year, as if each of us had felt afraid to betray the slightest hint of this event. I note it down here today. Now that we have learnt how to lose ourselves and each other in so many ways, we have nothing left to lose. The challenge of time has no hold on us now.

When we reached the bedroom, Martial stripped off his clothes. 'In my bare skin, like the first time you came to the farm!' He flung himself down on the unmade bed, punching the pillows, stroking the sheet, stretching his arms out over his head and clapping his hands as though to applaud himself: 'Come on, we'll all go to sleep together.' You stood for a long time turning your back on us, gazing out at the gardens through the shutters. Undressing slowly, I carefully folded my clothes, a habit I had long given up. Then I went up to you. Martial was watching us, surprised. Hadn't we followed him upstairs at once, quite spontaneously? It was then I unbuttoned your shirt. You muttered that we must be mad. I grinned and went to lie on the bed. Martial at once flopped over on his belly, closing his eyes, pretending child-like to be fast asleep. You joined us. Martial lay between us. He stirred a little, brushed against you, then touched my arm with his hand. Flat on our backs, you and I lay there staring at the ceiling. Now and again I glanced at you, but you never moved a muscle. The boy had his eyes shut tight. Forcing himself. A hornet found its way into the room and we watched it flying round a long time. Nothing happened. An ordinary siesta.

At midday Clothilde asked me: 'That was Martial at the funeral, wasn't it? Why didn't he come and say hello to me?' That's all.

Clothilde has just started playing the piano. The house is breathing again. You are breathing again.

# Fourteenth day

The ritual of the siesta was a kind of reward. Martial was always ahead of us. Every time he says: 'It's a secret', as if he alone had a feeling of danger. For him it was not so much a question of being taboo, it was sacrilege. Joseph would say, if he was waiting for him: 'Little Polyeucte is late today.'

Since I laid this notebook down yesterday, I gave myself twenty-four hours before resuming it today, feeling obliged to fill in the furrows of those three years. And I can't get that child's body out of my mind, that slippery smooth virgin body, wriggling, insinuating, the growing body of Martial which time and our actions sculpted almost before our eyes. The amazing growth of that boy! He stretched up, filled out and hardened, as though moulded by us. We watched and felt him grow, as if contact with us had enabled him to tap various springs of vitality and strength within us. And whatever we gave him he took like a thief. It was never a game, more like plunder or loot. It was war we were playing at.

As eight seasons passed, our siesta became a rite, a recreational break punctuating each and every day. Stockstill, Tityre would often stand at our bedroom door and stare intently at us. Or maybe he would sit, sphinx-like, watching our altar-bed with never-closing eyes, studying as the days slipped by the increasing intensity and deliberation of our movements. How much time elapsed before Martial became truly conscious of our bodies? There were three of us there, touching and hugging, brushing lips against cheeks and hands, grasping each other by the hair or the nape of the neck. A long period of little touches, of shy restraint. I remember Martial murmuring: 'Do I smell of hay?' Or this perhaps: 'I've got cobwebs in my hair. Last night I slept in the barn. In there I feel I'm with you already. Not at home any more. Some time I'll come and spend the night, a whole night here! That would be fun!'

All I can do is reconstruct. It is hard to fix an essence in words. Fixers of perfume are a rare breed and, like gold, perfume is a precious substance. Martial's use of language certainly lacked the fluency of form and almost conventional maturity that I have just assigned to it. But my memory is flawed. I think of Martial as he was at that time. I can see his smile as he snuggled into the tiny space between us, reminding us of the smell of the hay or the straw in that barn halfway from home where he preferred to spend his nights. And everything to him was fun. That was his way to proclaim without hypocrisy, though unable to define it, the true nature of his desires.

At a time when Joseph and I, in our thirties, had reached a degree of reciprocity that had led us to discover all manner of violent excesses in the way we used our bodies, Martial suddenly intervened, Hydra-like, between us. He was like a beacon of light to us, constantly haunted as we were by death and dark imaginings. He inflicted all sorts of siestas upon us, stifling summer siestas and freezing winter ones. We were on the way to becoming a carapace for him, his cocoon. And when in the evening we came face to face with each other again, alone, that child still lay between us. We began to treat each other with respect, as though an overheated embrace might have accidentally stifled the lurking boy who had chosen to lodge his raw desire in us. For till the very last day it was crystal clear that Martial had determined to make his nest with us.

We received no word from his parents, apart from those baskets which Martial would bring back from La Sarriete, stuffed with jams and mushrooms, and ringdoves ready dressed and barded with bacon, bottles of old Armagnac and the day's fresh butter and eggs. And when on occasion we took Martial home for the pleasure of the walk or to pacify him when he objected to returning, his parents would no longer greet us like benefactors or landlords, but rather with that silent gravity that betrays a human reluctance to own up to connivance. We taught Martial to read and write and gave him instruction, but that meant nothing to his parents compared with what Martial was turning into with us: a human being, already almost fully-fledged! Now, at the farm, the wild boy was no more. Martial would rise every morning at the first peep of dawn to go and work with his father, helping him so efficiently that Robert told us: 'Looks like you have to learn to read if you want to plough a good furrow.' The instinct that had prompted Martial's parents to hand their son over to us, with never an anxious thought as to where the relationship might lead, had this that was clear about it: it was free of moral stigma. No such thing as a suspicious mind in people like that. The land was their God, and we were directing their son's gaze back to them, towards their land.

Noting all this today, it seems to me that nothing is ever completely forgotten. Blotted out, that's all. Everything in life gets cancelled. Like a stamp or a date perhaps, but nothing in fact removes the enduring quality of time. The essential part of memories, what fixes them, is the initiating moment that first inspires, then marks and moulds. Only those who really know how to live accept this: whatever one achieves in life must be incomplete. In this way, from moment to moment, every little death becomes life. We have achieved an incompletion, Joseph, that is totally ambiguous.

And when we emerged from our bedroom, when it was time for Martial to go back home, only then would Tityre, mad with joy, rejoin us and jump on our shoulders to dig in his claws or rub his little cat face against our ears and our hair. How many times did Martial point out with a laugh that out of the four of us he was the only one *not* to have a moustache. 'You're all cats!'

Then, in the depths of the first winter, as if the icy wind had spurred us on, impelling each one of us towards the two others, the boy kissed us for the first time. Until then you and I had never embraced in front of him. We just lay there, containing ourselves, one on either side of him. That is all. Now he had kissed us. And soon these fumbling kisses led to gestures that for months had been held in check. Without prompting, it soon occurred to the boy to grab hold of us and wave us about. 'It's fun.' And when one day, bemused by it all, Martial watched me erupt, he was astonished and gravely stroked my belly, moving his little hand round in concentric circles. Now there had been a full demonstration. Another lesson in life. A new act was beginning. Now it only remained for him to grow and grow until he could explode like us. From then on the boy watched out for the first trace of hair on his upper lip, in his armpits, at the base of his belly and the springing of his thighs. That first day when he learned what an orgasm was, he turned to you, Joseph: 'And what about you?'

In the privacy of this study, in the silence of this house today, the fourteenth day since you died, I tell myself, Joseph, that we two are like a whole dying epoch and that after us life will be even more death-like. Righteous men have thought of a word to describe our conduct: scabrous. A word that has the ring of the gallows about it, the sound of a skeleton. A repressive word. A word that terrifies. But Martial was never terrified. Between us and him there was no premeditation. Only initiation. The great 'O' of his mouth was waiting for an answer and we gave it. Our pleasure was nothing if not his desire, the little rogue in our flesh.

A boy grew to manhood between us. In the proper sense. And the sense is aptly qualified.

In the room next to this study I can hear Clothilde changing the sheets on the bed. I wonder why?

123

She has just come in to say: 'You're sleeping here tonight, aren't you? You'd like to?' She smiled and explained: 'As you used to?' Then she slowly closed the door. You see, Joseph, incompletion is all. Nothing gets forgotten. Everything that is blotted out subsists.

# Fifteenth day

Joseph! I have just had a dream. I could see the dead digging deeper and deeper down into their tombs. That is how the whole dream started. I could hear the sound of the picks and the shovels scraping against the stones, as though all the inhabitants of a cemetery so vast as to encompass the earth, exasperated by the ever-increasing pace at which the living lead their lives this century, had decided to delve still further into the ground. It was a dark soft night with no wind. And skyless. With you conducting all that world of ghosts, marking the beat for every blow struck with a note from your deep bass voice. And like a voyeur I was there to champion the cause of those one still takes to be alive. You pretended you could not see me. I awoke trembling and sweating in bed, face up, with my neck arched back and my hands laid flat on the sheet, a rough clean sheet, a field of snow, a sheet of ice I was struggling to hang on to. But there was nothing to get a grip on and giddily I felt I was slipping. I could still hear your voice when I woke up, thudding away, descending lower and deeper, as if you too wanted to escape. Is that true? Where were you last night? With all those dead people?

And here I am severed from you, Joseph, mortified, toiling once more over this notebook, doubled in half as if someone had stuck a knife in my stomach. If I stop writing, the wound is likely to prove fatal. Every capital letter at the start of every sentence, every comma, verb or full stop assists in my convalescence. Understand me, Joseph, I *need* to tell our story. Our one virtue, our unique *raison d'être* lies in the fact that we shared the same desire and

125

were able to assume it, whereas in our own times, in our century, everything tends to be quantified and codified, evaluated even, in terms of predictable success. What we have lived lives still and will go on living on the fringe of all laws and all morality, wherever men or women accept themselves for what they are and know that this is never enough.

Oh, what a raging thirst and appetite we had for all the things on this earth, when the whole world stopped outside the gates of Saint-Pardom and left us free to rediscover in Antiquity a whole legacy of human culture which was to be frittered away through the dominance of a man who was crucified. And they exploited him all right!

It was a good dream I had, that burial ground where the dead were so busy escaping even further from the teeming ironical world of the living. Life: a whole world of people screaming to be heard, their minds set on conversion!

The point of these writings, as you know, is neither to excuse nor to glorify the more colourful events in our life, which is like the life of any other couple in touch with reality, any more than it is to mix falsehood with truth. in some place or other we are born unconvertible, and so at once cling to each other because there is nothing else to hang on to. And also perhaps, being comfortably off, because we had it in our power to do so. But money was never an end in itself for us. We were never in the slightest bit possessive about anything or anyone at all, not even one another.

In the charnel-house of my dream one fear took hold of me: that I might betray you or betray us. But in this notebook my urgent need is in fact to resuscitate myself, mouth to mouth, word by word, in order to survive, without you, whatever time may bring. To live out time past and, at the same time, time present. And at odd moments try to fish up those feelings on the fringe of memory which still await recall. How ongoing it all is, this going on with you! One last ramble. One grand tour! But there will be no more weddings at Montestruc and no bridegroom to greet us at sunrise.

When Clothilde knocked at the bedroom door, puzzled not to see me up and about, and announced that it was midday already and we were lunching at Copeyne with Sabine, she tapped so loudly on the wood that I thought my heart was being ripped out. It was such a long time since I had slept in that bed. Lying on that sheet, that virgin territory, on *your* side, in the place you always used to occupy, for the first time I really felt forsaken, and guilty for being there. Leaping out of bed with an aching head, I staggered into the study: I had to grab for this notebook so as to recover and get my breath back, to stop the thumping of my heart.

Then I slipped quickly beneath a shower of ice-cold water. There too I was alone. The curtain brushed against me and I shivered. It was the way you caressed me when you used to join me. Am I allowed to make a note of that? Who is there to observe me writing to you here, when all this anyhow is just between ourselves? Could there really be a judge in this house, watching and criticizing as I write, forgetting the inordinance of violent emotions when they are stirred by sentiment.

There I go, inventing the word inordinance for you – none of the other forms seemed quite right – as though at this point in my fight for deliverance I needed to invent a new language into which to translate our old one, that language of silent glance and gesture which was ours when we guardedly watched each other as Martial polished himself up against us. Today I must speak of Martial and tell the end of the story, or the end perhaps of this act in our lives. The event that was about to throw into turmoil everything within and around us.

Shortly after our meal Sabine announced the impending visit of a serious purchaser. Serious for her means wealthy. We had eaten our lunch in the pantry, for it would not have done to risk spoiling or dirtying the house, which had to be kept spotless, inviting, at

127

its best. Clothilde seemed not so much amused by this as bemused by my silence and the way I looked at her, so that she appeared to be floundering in the same helpless confusion into which I had been thrown by my visionary dream. Later, back here, she turned to face me at the foot of the stairs, rose up on tiptoe and, pressing her hands flat against her breasts, she gave me a little peck on the mouth, almost a kiss, and whispered: 'Don't be afraid, Roland, keep on going as you are . . .'

And now, as I prepare to set down this account of the departure of Martial, I cannot help feeling troubled by Clothilde's impulsiveness, by this house insidiously closing in upon me, as if I were afraid of its walls and the objects inside them. Disturbed too by the oppressive thought that some things which happen in the past are not bound to conform to conventional codes and modes, so that we may escape them, even if life leaves us behind. In this place and time of sexless quietude I turn to an already moulded past, unfolded yet still unfolding, to clasp it bodily and hug it to me as we used to hug each other.

That first day of March 1912, the news had spread like wildfire that Sullivan had been defeated by Georges Carpentier. The European middle-weight championship had taken place at Monte Carlo. The French champion had knocked out his opponent in two rounds, earning himself by that easy victory a title which delighted Martial. Martial was thirteen. Privately you and I had decided to let him go to our old college, in order to study for his Baccalaureat. Though not premeditated, it was an attempt to salvage him! Martial had learnt everything from us so quickly and with such enthusiasm that even in our own field of knowledge he had captivated, captured, ambushed us. Everything fascinated Martial and he was outspoken about it. He was mad about travel, and when we explained to him that only once in our lives had we ever gone away, on our trip to Taormina, he would fling at us: 'You'll never take me with you, I know you won't', or maybe 'What's the difference between travel and going away?' And neither of us would answer. We were only too anxious to stay put, as though jealously afraid of breaking any of the links that had tied the three of us together. Martial often used to tease us. He specially enjoyed reading to us those pages in the papers that dealt with trivia or items about sport, as if to thumb his nose at us, administer a shock or give the impression he was smashing his way out of our charmed triangle. So he had been struck by the story of Paul Cousin, the grocer's boy who, in order to create a scandal and generally upset his parents, had one afternoon in the Mollien Gallery of the Louvre slashed Nicolas Poussin's painting *The Flood*. 'Gosh! I think he's great! Cousin's a real brother to me!' he said, to provoke us. 'What was it like, that picture?' I described it to him. Martial was even more ecstatic. 'A beautiful picture! That's better still! Give me a knife!' How many times too did Martial act out the death of Watcher at the controls of his aeroplane when, during an important airshow at Rheims, that pilot, who had only been flying two months and had insisted on going up in spite of the bad weather, barely reached an altitude of 200 metres before he went into a nosedive and came crashing to the ground. Then Martial would point his hand and bring it plunging down on the dinner table. 'I want an aeroplane, I want to fly too . . .' But after our siesta had been going on for years, if we were a little late and kept him waiting, then he would call to us from the bedroom in his clearest voice in a tone of true anticipation. The one adventure he was really looking forward to was his first orgasm. That day was soon to come.

Throughout the meal Martial had been giggling and banging his hands on the table. Several times he had stood up and, holding up his fists right opposite you and me – do you remember, Joseph? – he had pretended for a joke to be Sullivan getting knocked out, and then Carpentier with his arm raised in triumph as thousands of hands gave him an ovation. 'Come on, don't sit still, you must stand up and clap him too!'

I went into the bedroom first, with Martial. You followed us. Tityre was asleep on the bed, but Martial pushed him off it. 'Get off, you lap-of-luxury cat!' It was the first time Martial had ever pronounced such a phrase. Tityre wouldn't move, so Martial picked him up and threw him out on to the landing. Then he closed the door and, still pretending to be a boxer, ripped his pullover and his shirt off. He punched me in the stomach and hit you in the face. You defended yourself and there we were all three of us jokingly engaged in a fight, which ended with the two of us pinning him down on the floor, you by the ankles and me by the wrists. 'You were bound to win! There are two of you!' Arching his back, he stretches and strains. Kneeling at the foot of the bed we have him nailed to the parquet. He struggles to get away. Furiously. Then he gives up. But only to try again, as if with one great jerk he might free himself. But we have firm hold of him. You look at me and I look at you, and at that moment for the first time it occurred to us both that Martial was now prey to us. The dismay born of recognition made us bear down with all our strength on the boy's arms and legs in order to fix him and the intensity of this moment by ensuring that inevitable outcome: with that down on his upper lip, those timorous hairs by the breast-bone and that bush at the base of his sex, now an extended quivering finger, gorged with blood. Giggling and gasping, Martial shouts abuse at us and then with another laugh he arches up more violently and suddenly erupts in spasms, two or three vigorous spurts that reached up to his neck and his face. Martial is shrieking, still twisting and turning, until he quietens down and lies still, his head rolling to one side, his eyes closed. He holds his hands over his genitals, then wipes his chin, his cheeks and his nose, and grins. A grin that turns into a sigh. Or a kind of grunt.

We remain kneeling, our hands on our knees, you and I facing one another, helpless, feeling guilty, not daring to look at each other. I suddenly feel excluded by this child who is no longer a child. What have I done? What have we done? This gushing ejaculation, his first, striking Martial in the face, is a strange and bitter sap addressed to no one but himself. I would rather not have seen, not have lived through that. It made an open wound, a gash that would get bigger and bigger through all that time still to come, Joseph, a gaping ever-widening gulf which will separate us and in the end has swallowed you up first and bides its time for me. Another fresh start, like one's first orgasm. Mankind is obsessed with seed-time. But is it really an obsession? This text is a gestation.

Martial turns over on his side, first one way then the other, as if he were rolling in a field, drunk with the new-mown hay. As though the house had started to pitch and toss before the shipwreck that would trap and drown us. Martial slides across the parquet and reaches out for his clothes. He gets dressed, still sitting on the floor, striking it from time to time with his fists. He has turned his back on us. He is going away. We know he is. We also know that he will not return, that he will never come back: he has had his orgasm, end of game.

He knows how to read and write and dream about travels abroad which may help him, who knows, to blur the memory of us, but never quite to efface it. He leaves the room, banging the door as he goes, and as usual you stand up and go to take your post by the window, where you contemplate through the slats in the shutters the stone vases disposed along the terrace, the neat gravel paths and the garden chairs turned upside down on the table in expectation of the promised showers. We can hear Martial on the floor below furiously opening and closing doors, as though he were pursuing someone. Then I walk up to you and make a gesture. I place my hand on your shoulder. You shake it off. I try to look you in the face. You turn your head away. I try to talk to you and several times I murmur your name, but you tell me to go away. I get dressed in my turn. I leave the room. I have the feeling it was only yesterday that Martial first arrived. All that time of restraint, all that devouring time, and then to be caught unawares by this ejaculation. Another birth. I can see him again that first day, pushing the pantry door open, carrying that basket. Joseph and Roland, he calls us. A cry for help, as I see it. It all began with an irruption. An eruption ended it. Martial is going away. The well of the staircase is strangely silent. The stairs seem to creak more than usual. The drawing-room door stands open as does the piano, abandoned, as if for several years now, unmindful or else bewitched, you had forgotten to sit down and play it. First I go down the steps on to the terrace. You are watching me, I can sense it, from the window of our room. Some people, Joseph, for love of one another, decline into disgrace. They don't destroy one another, they just deteriorate. Disdaining them, you and I *have* destroyed each other. But with no disgrace, we have spared ourselves that verdict. Here I stand stupefied, with you gazing down on me, wondering if Martial could have gone through the iron gates, leaving them wide open in his flight, abandoning Saint-Pardom to the buffeting of wilder winds than the breeze that crowned him with ruffled hair that first day to seduce us. It is with no exaggeration that I describe the sounds and the light and the events of that day. The ice-cold March sky banked with finely-etched clouds had at midday something of the pallor of its birth, brilliant, silent and righteous as the dawn. The whole park seemed petrified by the same astonishment that we felt.

I walk round the outside of the house. I try to call Martial by his name, but it gets trapped inside me, nagging at me deep down, stillborn or forgotten. I cross the kitchen-garden. All at once I feel sure that this is the way he went. Out through that door, *our* door, like a thief. When it comes within sight, half-open, behind a clump of plum trees, I stop and sit down for a moment on the rim of the well and, resting my elbows on my knees, I knead my face with both hands as if trying to force up the tears. To burst and gush forth too! And I strike the stonework with my fist just as Martial had beaten his against the floor of our room. Murder at the foot of a bed. Everything human turns to ritual.

I walk back to the house and push open the pantry door. Like that first day when Martial came surging in. On the big kitchen table Tityre is lying on his side, with a knife stuck clean through his stomach. He is still moving.

# Sixteenth day

Our children-to-be were never our children. We had only one brother: Sandro. And one son: Martial. The human family is mainly a matter of chance. This attempt to deliver our story to posterity will not deliver us from our past. Everything is governed by chance, from the notes we snatched from one another on the quiet to the many looks that have passed between us. You spying on me behind the shutters of our room. You watching me from afar on the platform of Cazauban station that wonderful day when I came back. You a choirboy at our good Fathers' Communion Service, holding the platen under my chin and winking. You waiting for me to wake up, placing one finger on my lips to prevent me opening my mouth. You on the terrace of the Café du Commerce saying that all these political arguments put one off politics completely. You begging me to come to our room as soon as I can, to join you. And the heavy tread of my footsteps on the stairs. As heavy as the look you then gave me. You pinned me down beneath you with your eyes, just as the two of us together pinned young Martial to the floor by force of arms.

Just now, shortly before dinner, Sabine came and brought us a basket, a kind of picnic. Father and Mother Bérard, she said, had invited her round for a chat on her own. Without irony: Sabine could not manage that. Face to face, it was as much as she could do to disguise the vexation she felt, seeing me back at Saint-Pardom, working and sleeping there. Moreover, one unfortunate word or gesture from Clothilde and she was ready to strike her sister. But the triumphal progress of her affairs obliged her to restrain herself. No doubt the Bérard parents are busy settling with their elder daughter the financial problems with which neither Clothilde nor I wish to be concerned.

Sabine was elegantly dressed. She too is coming out of mourning. She was wearing a dark mauve frock. I had never seen her in it before and, being too tight at the waist, it made her look stiff and doll-like. Could it be said, reading between these lines about Sabine, that I write of her with a kind of tender indifference? Tender at a distance. I leave Sabine strictly alone with her caskets of jewels and her dowager corsets.

Before she left us, anxious not to be late because of a *soufflé* that threatened not to wait, she turned to me and simply stated: 'Surrelac's son is buying Copeyne. The solicitor wants to see you tomorrow morning. At eleven o'clock.' Then she switched to Clothilde: 'Try and get him up in time. I've never been able to.' And wrapped in the splendour of this parting shot, she was about to sail down the steps, head high, when I caught up with her, swung her round by the wrist and, presenting her with a frank and open smile, murmured: 'When did I say I wanted to part with Copeyne?' 'Ah! that's it!' she answered. Then she tried to break away. I held her back and again I murmured: 'When did I talk about going to live in Paris?' 'Ah! That's it!' she repeated, and turned to her sister: 'Tell him to let me go!' Clothilde looked at me. I released Sabine. She took a few steps forward. Then suddenly spun round and pointed her finger at me. 'You thief!' Thief? Clothilde had just motioned to her sister to stop. Sabine broke into a laugh and made straight for the iron gates, which she shut with a clang by way of reprisal.

Back in the pantry, Clothilde is asking whether I want dinner in the dining-room. I answer with a non-committal 'No', still mightily intrigued by the combative air of Sabine, an assurance she lacked a few days ago, and this revelation of a different face which no longer expressed a resigned if almost haughty acquiescence, but a desperate drive for anything that might beget a rise in

134

status and distinction. Sabine's charm had suddenly been overlaid, as if a flush had spread over her cheeks, a harmless rash grown red and angry. At the sight of us together Sabine started playing her role in an adultery drama.

Clothilde opens the picnic basket. Stale bread, dried fruit and a cheese. Clothilde enjoys checking again and again the items that make up these paltry rations. She comes to me, extends a hand and lays it on my brow. 'You ought to be laughing too, Roland, it's very funny.' 'Don't say that . . .' 'Why, what's wrong? You look pale.' Clothilde is stroking my hair, as though she were trying to comb it. 'You'll tell me everything one day, won't you? Promise?' 'Promise!'

I sit down at the pantry table. I can still see Tityre, lying there stabbed. I caress the wood with the tip of my finger, searching for the nick, like a scar. But the wood has been washed and waxed, scrubbed and polished over so many years, again and again. It has grown quite smooth. However, I hold out my hand. Tityre is still moving slightly. I stroke him. He miaows. Tiny little miaowings that he would make when stalking birds under the lime tree. Joseph would shout: 'Call Tityre, he puts me off my reading.' I have no sooner left the terrain of my notebook than I am here at the real scene of the crime reported in the pages just completed. 'Now what are you doing?' Clothilde puts the plates and the glasses down on the table. I stroke the wood with the flat of my hand. I raise it to caress our cat, our attic hunter, our little Jack-in-the-box, always popping up out of the nearest basket. I wait for him to die. He is dribbling a little. And his blood makes a small pool round his stomach, sticking to his fur. Laid on his side, Tityre's eyes are fixed straight in front of him, gazing at the window. I lean over so that he can see me. The look in his eyes troubles me. That stare. The stare of all those years spent watching us through the bedroom door or sometimes, when he would push it open with his nose and come in, from the bedside table on which he would jump to observe all three of us. All three

135

of us! Then with one motion I pull out the knife. One convulsion and Tityre is dead.

'What on earth are you doing . . .' Clothilde grasps my hand. I look at her and smile. 'Nothing. Really, I promise you, it's nothing.' And I kiss her on the brow. We sit down at the table and quietly have dinner. Now and again Clothilde glances at the wooden table and then at me, questioningly.

Immediately after dinner I came back up here. Clothilde is at the piano, trying to sight-read the first piece in *Favourite Classics*. Diabelli's eternal Sonatina. And I am writing this in memory of Tityre. And in memory of Martial. This is the second time this evening that I have pulled that dagger out. My memories race ahead of me and drag me after them. But who will drag this fountain pen from my fingers?

# 13 March 1912. From Joseph.
## The Invitation

Madame Bérard wants to look round the gardens. Her daughters stayed with Roland and their father in the drawing-room. She rose to her feet, took me by the arm and said: 'Let's go and see all the things you grow!' directing a glance at her husband to make it plain that she wished to be alone with me.

So we walked, she leaning on my arm and I hurrying her along. I try hard to lead her back into the house, but no, she *will* see everything. By the lime tree: 'Isn't it beautiful!' By the evergreen oaks: 'How big they are!' By the privet hedges: 'Who trims them?' And between the hedges, just by the kitchen-garden, that patch of earth so recently dug over: 'It looks like a grave!' 'Precisely, Madame, that's where we buried our cat.' She looks at me in surprise, slightly perplexed. 'Your cat? But a dead cat, you just throw it out!' I make no reply.

In the vegetable garden she stands stock-still. I move on as if I had not noticed. Two more steps and her hand has slipped out of my arm. Now we are detached from each other. I take a breath and turn to look at this sharp-eyed woman with the decisive gestures, all dressed up for a social call. She is smiling. 'You know, Joseph – you don't mind if I call you Joseph, do you? – I used to know your mother a little. She never talked very much about you, but she was very fond of you . . .' Madame Bérard draws closer and tries to take my arm again. I move away, my hands behind my back, and start walking again. She keeps her distance but follows me: 'Shouldn't we talk about the purpose of our visit? You would

137

never have stayed such a long time here in this town, you and Roland, if you hadn't intended one day to marry Sabine and Clothilde! Clothilde will be ideal for you. And Sabine and Roland will make a lovely pair. Look me in the face! You're not shy, are you?' I halt next to the well. Madame Bérard sits down on the rim, adjusts the folds of her dress and strokes the rings on her fingers. 'Roland has his qualifications. That's very nice for Sabine. As for you . . .' This time I look Madame Bérard straight in the eye. Is she going to start on about Rigand? Does she think of me as an unfrocked priest? She says no more. Then she began to sing the praises of the garden: 'Your mother really looked after it well.' And then she went on in a low voice, holding out her hand for me to help her up: 'Don't blame *me*! After all, it's the same choice you made at Montestruc, six years ago already! Everyone has to get married!'

Making our way back to the house, she takes my arm again. She clings to it, punctuating every sentence she speaks with a little squeeze of her hand conspiratorially. 'And May is the month for weddings. Two on the same day, that will be perfect!' There was something in the way she pronounced the word 'perfect', a sharpness, a meanness, which was to colour the rest of her conversation until we parted company.

We return to the drawing-room, where Roland is bringing in the tea. Monsieur Bérard stands up. 'You've been a long time!' Madame Bérard takes her seat in the armchair by the chimney-piece and looks at her daughters with an air of satisfaction. 'Well, Roland, now you can kiss Sabine! And you, Joseph, kiss Clothilde!'

As he sets the teapot down on the tray, Roland knocks over a cup. Madame Bérard gazes at each of us. 'We're waiting!' Roland stares at me. I hold out my hand to Clothilde. He holds out his to Sabine. Both the girls stand up. And we kiss them on the brow. Madame Bérard claps. 'Wonderful, I'm so happy!' Monsieur Bérard is standing stiff and straight by the fireplace, his thumbs in his waistcoat pockets, his paunch sticking out. He consults his watch. Madame Bérard is jubilant. 'Well, girls, now you can serve the tea and show your fiancés that you have manners too.'

If I note all this down, the brief premeditated statements, the well-calculated gestures, the strange proprieties, it is out of amazement at the ease and rapidity with which human beings take refuge in the social norms, when some desperate expedient has given them a glimpse of the splendid risks involved in giving way to their emotions. Or to passion. *Idem*!

During this visit to Saint-Pardom everything apparently went according to plan. But deep down in the two of us, Roland, everything is under siege, disarming and alarming us. So immediately, as if alerted by Martial's departure, we have had to run round to the Bazaar more frequently than usual to furnish ourselves with all kinds of things which we suddenly imagined ourselves to be in need of. Only to come to the conclusion that we were neither of us averse to becoming sacrificial victims to the rites of marriage. Not by way of escape, but in order to alter something that for several days had become all too clear: that the picture we sent back to each other was no longer the dazzling image we had of ourselves in our twenties. A stage in our lives had perhaps just ended as well. The choice of these two sisters, however much it appears to make a concession to the accepted conventions of life in our town, is for all that none other than a clandestine method by which to espouse each other officially. Thereby establishing, as Madame Bérard might say, that we too are not without manners!

Since the departure of Martial we no longer dare to throw our arms about each other. Martial has even run off with that desire too. He has stuck his knife in everything. When furtively I kiss you, as if to give some encouragement or seek some comfort for myself, I close my eyes because you close yours, too. One part of our lives is over. The Bérards have paid us their neighbourly visit at last. And the game is up.

139

Clothilde is pouring out the tea. 'One sugar or two? A drop of milk?' Sabine serves Roland first. Madame Bérard is talking about Copeyne, which she would like to visit. Monsieur Bérard sets his cup down on the mantelpiece. Politely munching a biscuit, he is looking round at the pictures, furniture and other objects. He will only speak once, in order to ask me to play the piano: 'And you manage to find the time for music?' Perfectly friendly all this, but always on the brink of disapprobation. Madame Bérard casts a broody eye over her daughters, as though she had reserved them especially for us. I try to imagine what it means for her, her day of triumph. While I am improvising a whimsical little waltz, so that they should not enjoy a favourite piece of *our* music, I can hear Roland stirring his tea indefatigably with his teaspoon. A little tinkle. I know, Roland, that you are there behind me, rejoicing at the thought that I have not selected a piece known to us and to us alone, music that we have shared. Our first connivance.

Then they rose to their feet. We accompanied them to the gates, flanking Mother and Father Bérard, one on each side. Sabine and Clothilde were following behind. Now and then we would turn round to smile at them. And at each other. Our second connivance.

And here from the study I am watching you. I have left the bedroom door open. You are stretched out on the bed. I can hear you turning the pages of a book. I imagine you smoothing your moustache, moistening the tip of your finger to place it at the top of the right-hand page, and frowning because something in the text, a word, an idea or an opinion has diverted and surprised you. You are waiting for me.

After the Bérards had left, we never exchanged a single word. Not even during dinner, which was rushed through and soon over, as though we felt the need to seek asylum again in our two first-floor rooms at Saint-Pardom, now that the day's infamy was complete. We looked at each other and grinned, as though what had just happened had caught us by surprise. A visit that would last a lifetime! The downward slope on the other side. Now everything will move faster! After all, Madame Bérard's logic is irrefutable. If we have lingered on in this town, it must be on account of Clothilde and Sabine. When a cat dies, you throw it out!

You are waiting for me. But I need to write it down: what this means is another fresh start, even more than when we first became wrapped up in one another. I need to state quite clearly that there will never be a day when our differences fail to become more marked, marking and accusing us, when everything that divides us, now and in the future, will stop tightening its hold on us, threatening to throw us into a struggle that will steadily grow more violent and more desperate.

I cannot help thinking this evening that we have opened a gate that will never close. From now on the whole town will be the depository of our secret. We have reached such a level of despair that any form of hope is valid. We enter their lives, but we shall keep ours to ourselves. They are simply paying us a visit. A different sort of desire will take root in us, Roland. An effusiveness in our reserve. A holding back as sly as our most recondite caresses. I was surprised by the sensitive way you kissed Sabine on the forehead, just as you must have noticed the kiss I planted on Clothilde's. Such marks of tenderness do nothing to diminish our ardour. To go on battling with each other, though this time without touching, will not be betraying anyone! As a couple we stand alone. You wait for me, just as I, writing in here, wait for you. This evening we shall reinvent all kinds of gestures for our isolated bodies, now that Martial has cloven us in two. Perhaps we shall find a way to banish the hollow left by that child between us. I am sure of it even. I can sense a fresh savour, like new sap rising within me.

I saw Robert this morning at market. He shook me warmly by the hand and asked me to thank you. 'I am proud of my son,' he said, 'thanks to you two!' I forgot to tell you before, because already there seemed to be no point. There was such a ringing tone in

Robert's voice, a supreme transparency that had a deeply human quality. And it generated inside me a great desire for you again. But different. More remote.

I am coming to join you and lie down beside you. It still remains for us to explore the greatest river in the world. Parallel bodies in this bed, our canoe!

# Letters for a double wedding

Copeyne, 17 May 1912

Dearest friend and brother-in-law!
Dear Joseph,
Greetings from the old bear! Sweet was the night! I nearly forgot that we had promised to write to each other, this time as a real letter. Didn't we say we would exchange morning-after letters at the post-mortem on the wedding at old Mother Bérard's later on today? Have you written yours yet?

I was slow to wake up. Sabine was asleep on her side, in her nightgown, turning her back to me with her arms folded over her breasts. I slipped out of bed. This house at Copeyne is really foreign to me. I made the parquet floor creak as I stole to the window. Sabine did not move. I quietly pushed the shutters open. It was like Montestruc! But the sun was fully risen, it wasn't dawn this time. Perhaps we should have got married sooner?

Sabine is agreeable. Knowledgeable almost. She must have read a few manuals, or had rather too long to wait. Submissive, yet with no false modesty, she tries to impress and subjugate me. And since it is only sensible in the context of this letter that you should know how it all went, let me tell you in all frankness that I was fully regaled.

In some of her movements Sabine was as awkward as I was, but in others she was disarming, unerring and exciting. And since

143

yesterday's events have obliged you and me to accept conventions of every kind, including linguistic ones, I can tell you that our marriage has been consummated. Sabine is a queen bee now.

I know all this may sound devilishly ironical. But when I'm writing to you, my marriage seems to belong to another world. Or to put it more precisely, I am possessed by the idea that I got married twice! Were there not four of us facing the altar yesterday? Did it not occur to you as it did to me, that the Father Superior had forgotten to ask us to say Yes twice? Two additional Yeses, one from you and one from me? Just for us? What fun that would have been! Sorry, I ought to cross out the word 'fun'. There is someone between us can still claim it as his. After Martial, 'fun' isn't funny any more.

This must be one of those turning-points in a letter where one switches on to a more serious level. That wedding ceremony was in some minds a real celebration. A joyful one, with the sun participating, for all those people who over so many years have crossed our path, to be greeted or ignored, and who for one day became our friends. As if the whole town had joined together in rejoicing, in order to wipe out the memory of your mother and my father and restore their children to its bosom again. The important thing is that they believe it.

Sabine is still sleeping. I have time to go on.

So many charming friends, so many smiles, so many repetitions of 'I used to know your . . .' or 'We're so glad that at last you . . .' or 'Two wonderful couples you make. Congratulations. Here's to the next time, for the christenings!' Those were the wishes that stuck in my mind.

It has all happened so quickly! Only this morning I realized that in fact, during all those years of withdrawal, every time you went to our bedroom window you were looking out at the town, interrogating it. I'm not trying to accuse you of remorse, am I?

144

Ours is an honourable love, since we still honour it ourselves. Oh, how unsettled I am this morning! My sentences won't hang together. My heart is beating too fast. And I'm trembling a little. But you are bound to notice that when you read this letter. This is not my handwriting.

I shall note down a few things at random. The two of us waiting in the choir of the cathedral for our brides to arrive a little late, only the two of us in front of the altar for quite a long time, and the bells pealing out as we emerged into the square, I first with Sabine, the elder sister, and you following behind.

For the first time I walked in front of you. Perforce.

Sabine is still sleeping. I have the time. As soon as she moves, I shall stop.

That day of tributes, pomp and elegance was agony to me. But agony makes suffering easier to support. All I know of my father is this one reflection he made shortly before he died: 'The misfortune is theirs, the pain is mine.' Happiness, misfortune! That's what they were playing at yesterday, all around us. Watching you, I was aware of the way you looked at me. We were terribly close to one another right through the day. And here we are inventing new embraces. Our imposed isolation will only sharpen our consciousness and our desires!

How handsome you looked! And how wonderful I felt! Utterly at ease. Our only limitation now is the horizon, forever receding as we advance. No longer independent in our interdependence, we belong somewhere else. Time is conniving with us. Yesterday, thanks to that mockery of a wedding, those farcical conventions, we stepped once and for all outside our own times into eternity. Yet I doubt if anyone realized that this ceremony was not our concession to society but our accession to communion of a different kind.

There was something sardonic about their celebrations.

Unpleasant even. Belonging to the past. A past with no hope of evolution. All those people reliving the old days, dead and gone, as a diversion. The only past we can generate now is a living past stretching ahead of us.

Perhaps you are expecting a factual letter couched in a pseudo-adult style of academic probity and irony that would trace a vivid picture of a day of great festivities and a night of lost virginities. What I am giving you betrays the beating of my heart and the feeling that I got up too late.

Sabine has just stirred, shifting a little from side to side. She is lying on her back, still in the nightgown she wore for her wedding night. With a red stain. She is holding her arms out to me. I must close.

And I sign this: your brother-in-law,
Roland.

At Saint-Pardom
17 May 1912

My Roland,
I am writing to you in haste, on the sly. Not that Clothilde is keeping her eye on me already, but the least I can say is that I spent a sleepless night, full of attentive little tokens of tenderness and affection. Clothilde continually fixed me with an open wide-eyed questioning look. Just at first I was intimidated. But when spontaneously she removed her bridal nightgown, with that obscene slit in the lace at the front, and came to kneel naked on the bed, bending forward with a friendly little laugh to draw the tip of one finger across my neck and my chin, then my nose and my forehead, we were both won over to each other.

Clothilde has just gone into the bathroom. As she jumped out of bed she grabbed her virgin nightdress to cover herself in modesty as she fled to the shower. And with a smile she whispered: 'I won't be long.' Amused, I answered: 'All the time in the world.' I like this complicity. There is no deceit here. I could be saying or writing this in order to convince myself. But that is not the case. My attraction to Clothilde is genuine, but of a different, special kind. This is what I discovered last night.

I dislike images, but somehow when you need them, you make use of them because they may be of help. What *we* love, the two of us, is overgrown bushes and woods. These are our parklands, our laid-out gardens. And it is no coincidence how punctiliously we raked the weeds from our gravel paths on the day of their visit.

Yesterday I had no sense of the grotesque or the sacrilegious. No other person could ever offer me excitement so engrossing as the natural simple joy of knowing you are at my side, embarked with me, as equals, on an adventure that started pure and simply with an escape and the murder of a cat. How long ago already? Barely three months?

I can hear the water from the shower. The familiar clatter. It doesn't trouble me. It is she, not you this time. Another person. A different one.

I was inside her almost before I realized. A new sensation, face to face! She practically bit me in the shoulder. And now the idea that she needs this water, as if she wanted a new body, perhaps – no surely – to come back to me, leaves me not without satisfaction, even if still unsatisfied. Inviting the reflection that a marriage of convenience does not always exclude a kind of desire. For company.

One single detail yesterday kindled my affection. I felt I was being pinned down, vainly fluttering my wings, when I caught the subtle perfume of Clothilde's circlet of orange blossom, as it wafted in waves pervasively around me. As soon as Clothilde came to take her position next to me in the cathedral choir the scent of those interwoven flowers seemed to draw me closer to

147

her. And if throughout the day I scarcely left my lady's side, it was this fragrance, you see, that bound me to her. Or attracted me rather. For I felt under no obligation. Quite simply I was happy.

Clothilde has just shut the water off. Quick, quick!

But why? No need for haste. I have left the door ajar between the bedroom and this study. Nothing to hide from Clothilde. And she knows how to use her eyes. I find her gaze disconcerting but arousing. Yes, it roused the gallant in me. Everything went off very well, thank you.

I choose this way to tell you, as I know you will not accuse me of vulgarity. When was it you said 'vulgarity is after all something you have inside you'? Like the urge to roam, an instinct for welcome or the truth! In fact we have it all inside us, don't we? Welcome is who welcome makes! Perhaps my eyes expressed welcome to Clothilde as well. A matter of orange blossom.

Interruption. Clothilde has just called me. 'I'm in here, Clo.' Clo? I never gave it a second thought. It just slipped out. She came into the study for a few moments, draped in the top sheet she pulled off the bed as she passed. And this is what we said: 'You're writing?' 'Yes.' 'What about?' 'About us!' 'Who to?' 'To Roland.' Silence.

She simply murmured, 'I envy you!' Then she took a step back, running her hand along one of the library shelves. She gave a happy little smile, a sort of pout, and then said in an even quieter voice. 'I feel like writing to Sabine too.' And then as she sneaked away, slipping softly through the doorway, I heard her whisper, 'But . . .' That was all.

There. Now she's humming. And as she seems not to have her eye on the clock, in spite of being a Bérard, and has granted me more time for this letter, I can now turn my attention to you.

The whole night long I forgot to think about you. That is the truth. The first night since Cazauban that I have not lived in or close to you; only the day before yesterday we spent our last evening as bachelors together, making a grand tour of the fields and the woods, side by side, with you grasping my hand or me taking hold of yours. *Quid faciat laetas segetes, quo sidere terram vertere, Maecenas, ulmisque adjungere vites conveniat* . . . What art is needed for the finest harvests? Under which stars, Maecenas, is it prudent to turn over the soil and marry the vineyard to the elm? You recited all this to me from memory and now I am translating it as if to breathe more life into our language by listening to the voice of the *Georgics*.

This morning a kind of fear has gripped me. Shall I have the courage to exchange this letter for yours if a sombre look tells me what you might try with a smile to conceal? Clothilde's 'But' has just begun to disturb me. I know that only the thought that my happiness was more frank and open than your own might make you put on your boorish look to cover up any disappointment you may feel.

And now, as I write, I am holding your hand and clasping you close to me. We are about to get married to the vineyard and the elm. You chose those verses, didn't you?

I embrace you with my whole self, body and soul. I can hardly wait to exchange our letters. And now I don't want Clothilde, my Clo, to grow anxious.

Tibi,<br>Joseph.

# 19 December 1913. From Joseph.
## The wind and the wave

I feel like a stream choked with slippery weeds smoothly trailing through the water. I am haunted by Clo's head of hair. At times I wake up entangled in it, convinced for a moment that her mane is strangling me. Now in my dreams the only oak trees I see are evergreen. Everything is terribly young and impatient to grow. In my dreams I don't walk any more. I am always motionless, observing that clump of young holm oaks. A frozen picture, a still life, I force myself to wake up. For I should so hate in my sleep, out of habit, to unnerve the girl who has taken your place with some brutal embrace. What have we done? What kind of revenge is this? On whom and for what?

And in my dreams I also imagine that if we came together again this whole rigid landscape would spring to life. Then I would remind myself that this is only a dream. Or have our two wives tapped all those forces of Nature around us which have always encompassed our lives and imposed their own rhythms upon us?

Clo is serene in her pregnancy. She talks a great deal about the child she carries within her. He's moving already, she says. Would it shock you if I confessed how then I long to tell her that you still move within me? But I refrain. Because that is not done. Instead, I write it down and pass it on in the secrecy of these pages, which like so many others before them will be consigned to the dark night of this dossier, our act of indictment in the sense that we still indict each other for confronting the absolute.

Oh, what devastating solitude in these pages! Is any joint creation possible outside the living reality of a couple? As I write I have the impression you are reading it all, lurking somewhere inside me: a feeling that never ceases to astound me. Have you stolen my eyes? And have you slipped my hands on like a pair of gloves? And what of my body?

Does Sabine talk to you of the child she is expecting? I pass straight from you to her as if her blank refusal to reveal any hint of the bond between you was somehow hurtful to me.

I bumped into Martial this morning in the market. He was delivering poultry and eggs. He waved to me from a distance, a high clear wave of the hand. He shouted 'Good morning'. Like a peal of laughter. That is all. He went on his way. And I went mine. And I went ours, for at every step we still trip over each other's feet. We have to admit, Roland, that we have not yet emerged from one another. We had too deeply merged together. But anything can happen in this world. And on every side the news is most alarming. In this century anything can happen, and the Devil knows there are plenty of possibilities. No doubt he will make good use of them. One thing only counts and will remain to bear witness: the fusion of us two.

We have conjured up the most extravagant images for ourselves. Not a day goes by without my remembering that boxing ring, a framework for our first design for living, a closed square of ropes from which we ceaselessly rebounded one against the other, round after round. When Martial raised his hand in recognition to greet me this morning, I could not help thinking of his joy on the great day of Carpentier's victory and his first orgasm. Martial was the referee who broke up our clinches, for ours was a well-matched fight that threatened to end in a double knock-out. Memories rope us off too, to stop us falling out and make us bounce back at each other. And so the pressure of these sentences, these notes, builds up an urgency in me to climb up to the attic, open the

151

dormer window from which I can see Copeyne and call out to you by name.

But Sabine would hear it as well. And my Clo would start worrying. She is not allowed to go upstairs any more. She sleeps in the drawing-room next to the piano, and sometimes when she can't sleep I sit down and play very quietly for the three of you: for her and the child and for you. Yes, you. Who is writing this? You or I? You are inside me, my stowaway!

Our meetings have become a strange ritual. Like a play in repertoire shown on alternate nights. One evening spent at Saint-Pardom, the next at Copeyne and so on. The two sisters compete in happiness with one another. I can't help being amazed at Clo's spontaneous effusions, when all Sabine's joys are so carefully doled out. She is too anxious, I feel, to keep her reproaches to herself. And a reproach withheld turns virulent, with limitless power to hurt. With Clo, I am ahead of you again. The order of precedence observed on our wedding day, when you and Sabine came out of the cathedral first, is simply the exception that proves our private rule. The genuine concord between Clothilde and me is merely feigned between you and Sabine. On reflection I have to admit that I am the only one to feel hurt by this. I know you are too resilient to suffer from it, and you know I am too impressionable not to be affected. Such a ricochet is part of our love too.

I love the wind in December, the keen air. It sets a distance between Saint-Pardom and Copeyne. This evening when we come over to you, putting a big woollen shawl round Clo's shoulders, I shall think of this love I still harbour and conceal within me. As soon as we arrive, the first glance we exchange will be our latest form of embrace!

Only one love, that is all. I die where I am tethered. I live where I am tethered. It all comes to the same. A motto for an embroidered handkerchief. We are as tenacious as ivy.

But when in the evening Clo loosens her bun and liberates her hair, it cataracts round her shoulders and I forget you, I erase you. She is all wave, whereas you remain the wind. She is tender love, far removed from violent passion. I love you, Roland. At last this is the right verb for us. Peace of mind inspires it. A sense of order. Distance.

She is all wave and you are the wind, always biting, harassing, lashing, now whipping these words along and chasing me away from these pages which you will read right through this evening at a glance. One look is enough. Says it all. An absolute masterpiece. Those terrible incomplete works of ours. Smile, then!

# 7 February 1913. From Joseph.
## Quite a couple

Henri was born yesterday at seven in the evening. Marie was born today at five in the morning. You simply had to have a son who would be older. And I had a daughter. A question of sensibility. Or is this yet another difference between us that helps to forge our likeness?

It all happened as if our two sisters had tipped each other off. But still observing precedence, Sabine was first! And how overjoyed you were: what pride as you arrived here out of breath shouting 'It's a boy!' Was that what set off Clothilde's labour pains so prematurely? All the midwife had to do was move from one house to the next.

Sabine never uttered a sound. You even told me that this made you anxious. They packed you off, didn't they, into the drawing-room at Copeyne? You told me how frustrated you felt. So I never confessed to you that at the last moment Clothilde called me into our bedroom. A noisy room of shouts and moans, and stuffy too, for they had heaped too many logs on the fire. Mother Bérard approached me as soon as I went in, incensed at my being there: 'This is not allowed!' She turned to the midwife who was getting Clothilde ready: 'Is it, Madame?' But Clo extended an arm, and so urgently that I went and took her by the hand. And there, standing over our bed, and I mean *our* bed, I found it hard, like Clo, not to shut my eyes. I found it hard breathing all that in, the damp stench of the overheated atmosphere, of pain! Clo punctuated her cries with convulsive pressure from her fingernails into the palm of my hand.

This is what Clo wanted. She had drawn me into it. I had to see it all! I watched the baby's slimy little head twisting out and the plump hands of a strange woman who kept repeating: 'Breathe, Madame, keep breathing in and out!' And I started breathing with Clo, in time with her. I was looking straight into her eyes. I no longer wanted to watch that newborn child painfully emerging. Then the midwife almost sang it out: 'It's a girl!' Clo screwed her face into what was almost a smile! She pulled me down to her and whispered indistinctly in my ear, repeating it several times before I understood: 'Open the window . . . open it.'

As I went to do so, Mother Bérard held me back: 'What are you interfering for!' And Clo almost shrieked: 'Go away, Maman.' Old Mother Bérard looked at her daughter, then at the midwife, who was cleaning up the baby, and stalked out. I opened the window. Clo had her eyes closed, breathing more calmly now. She had her second wind and fell asleep almost at once. I looked at the wriggling little thing that is ours. The midwife had gone to work without a smile, but so methodically I did not dare go near her. Then I began to breathe more freely like my sleeping Clo.

The night air is laden with dryness. The winter earth has an almost metallic smell. I draw strength from it and am amazed at so much tranquillity when scarcely an hour ago the whole house was screaming blue murder. All this noisy bustle and pain that surrounds a child's entry into the world seems to be sounding a warning. Thus all life begins with the cry of the dying: 'Oh no! Not that!'

When I went down to the drawing-room, there you were. You had returned after rushing backwards and forwards time and again between your house and mine. You said: 'Where were you hiding?' I gave no answer. That was my secret. I had seen. 'It's a girl.'

You stumbled back and bumped into a chair. You did not understand my smile. And you rushed off, furious. Why?

And here I am, writing. Installed in an armchair facing the bed. Our little Marie is asleep in a blanket. Frail, wrinkled. And only just now you were arrogantly proclaiming how many pounds your son weighed. 'And he's got some hair!'

Have we quarrelled for the very first time? How banal. Here I am, sitting up through the night, waiting for the dawn. For a little Henri, a little Marie, the dawn of their very first day. Will they ever learn how to live? I cannot repudiate the past. Everything alters us, that's all. As you ran away from me, you ran towards me and I, blind as ever, moved to meet you. And we collided. And now there are two children. Quite a pair, the two of us, quite a couple!

# Twenty-first day

June already! Almost like summer. I have just torn May from the calendar, Joseph, the month you died, peeled it off like a layer of dead skin. Twenty-two years later, having only just finished copying out the notes on Quite a Couple, I feel I must have my say. That night of the two births, all the toing and froing I did between Copeyne and Saint-Pardom, Saint-Pardom and Copeyne, seemed only to lengthen the distance between our two homes and fill it with pitfalls and hazards, as though the town had stretched out its tentacles of lane and wall, fence and hedge, to sequestrate us, two prisoners still enmeshed in one another. And then that silent emptiness! I hunted for you. Then not daring to go up to that first floor of shouts and cries, I went back to my house to find myself alone again, confined below, forbidden to go upstairs. I had caught no more than a furtive glimpse of my newborn baby, Henri, our first born. When Old Mother Bérard came back from your place, she said the same thing to me: 'Stay where you are. Don't *you* start interfering too!' And she had slammed the drawing-room door before I had the time to yell: 'Get the hell out of here!'

So I went out and took that perilous path again. Winding round my neck a scarf that I had snatched up in haste, knotting and unknotting it, I lashed out at the bushes and the walls, kicked the stones, waved my fist at the louring black sky and shouted at the wind to stop swirling and gusting through the trees as it sharpened its bite on the naked branches. I can still see it all now: the gnarled fingers of the fig-trees in silhouette, clutching out to grab me and deter me, mocking at my efforts to return to you again.

I had reached a state of exasperation. For slightly under a year we had been trapped in a nightmare. And all on account of a little boxer and a cat that was stabbed. After climbing the rising slopes of our lives clinging close to one another, triumphing over all that heaven and we ourselves could throw up to impede us, we had in our solitude reached the dominating heights. And all to end up like this. You, smiling and serene with Clo. And I coming and going, tangential to Sabine, dreading the downward slopes and the thought that being together now means only side by side, inventing fresh embraces that grow more and more abstract, like the fabrications of those who, for want of spirit, talk about love without ever having known or enjoyed it. People like that inhale the present and only exhale the past. They expire! But we two?

That night was hard and metallic. I have already mentioned the winds. They were distracted too. What had we just done? Committed? These children who were they, springing from us and emerging from these two sisters? What human soil had we just furrowed and sown? How far would our love for them take us? And would we be leaving them a dangerous legacy of improper pride with which to enter a world stubbornly bent on over-invention, on mastering and ruining everything, whereas we, opting out of the pressures of our age, had chosen what to some looks like indolence, but was in fact the greatest struggle life offers in reality? Had we just committed an injustice?

These were the questions I would have liked to ask you. But one smile from you unnerved me. And when you came down from our bedroom, proud and buoyed up to have 'seen' the birth of *your* firstborn, Marie, yet imbued with the same consciousness and as plagued as I was by the same interrogations, you chose not to give an answer.

That night of the two births I had a deep self-lacerating

consciousness of being, which pervaded everything inside me. The incoherence of my movements and my stubborn resolve to strike out at the stones and everything in my way on that path which now created such distance between our two separate homes, betrayed an urgent need for language in which to express myself. My blows were an interrogation. This repeated barrage of questions left a trail of destruction through the night. It would have taken little for me to use my scarf and hang myself: 'How funny, what fun!' as Martial would have said. There are times when to feel over-conscious of one's existence is to feel so unsupported that everything is insupportable. Oh, what power a fleeting emotion can have, when it deludes you to the point of performing a poetic act of justice on yourself.

Night, that great night of iron, tin and leaden dust, wind of mica and alumina: and I, master metal-worker, in search of my companion! Let us return to today. What a situation you have left me in!

Henri has passed his examinations. We heard two days ago. The reasons of the heart dictate, don't they Joseph, that I should not leave Saint-Pardom, not sell Copeyne, not follow Sabine and play the part she has cast me in, opposite her, in her comedy of manners? She wants me to go up to Paris to shape, model and mould her elder child into a wonder-boy. I shall follow her. I shall act out my role, but not one word will I say. I have no lines to speak. I shall become, for her as well as for my son, a husband and father whose very existence will soon be quite forgotten. I shall not be mentioned after my death. For me, to talk of Paris is to talk of dying. It spells anonymity, my last attempt to get back to you. I shall go in search of daggers. I know where they are to be found. Up there I shall encounter all those temptations I knew before, the year we were separated, at the time of your examination, the diploma you took for appearance's sake! Perhaps I shall follow Sabine in her move the better to remind myself that you are waiting for me. My death will come like a second rendezvous at Cazauban.

159

Reasons of the heart dictate, don't they Joseph, that I should stay on here with Clothilde? I have just caught her unawares with her long hair streaming down. She was brushing it slowly with youthful grace. The mere fact of my presence in this house seems to awake in her the odd gesture that strangely evokes the most intimate drama in this notebook, which in trying to reconstruct our lives may well perpetuate them. Yes, there is something perpetuating in Clothilde's attentiveness. She is pointing the way for us to follow. And if on that night of the two births I was dashing backwards and forwards, rather as I am in my writings today, perhaps it was also because I felt that, through her, you were less lonely than I was. Clothilde brushing her hair? The image comes to my mind of those streaming river weeds that proliferate in all the little brooks where we used to splash water at each other.

Henri has been successful. Now he will despise me even more. He is going to play society's little game, pretending to build up what it is busy knocking down, quietly cultivating under the cloak of liberalization a variety of conflicting moral codes, both religious and anti-religious. It all comes to the same in the end. Oh, to stay on the fringe! That was our way! In Paris, marginal to the others, I shall look for the end of the road, a railway station platform with a return to eternity. As all this makes no accepted sense, it must have significance.

I have already filed away the greater part of the notes you made for the work which you would probably have entitled: *Readings from Virgil*. I have also filed my own concerning Livy. Is it worth noting that in the watchful silence of our days together we accomplished all this work, devoted our whole life to studying the production of these two great poets? Now don't scowl! Livy is important to me. And all these notes are destined for the darkness of a drawer. I shall deposit them here until Marie, who will inherit this place, chooses to destroy them. Who knows? Or in a matter-of-fact way they may just get thrown out. After the style of Old Mother Bérard throwing out her cats.

160

Only this notebook will remain. And I shall hide that too. But just as Clothilde has not forgotten how to brush her hair, will she remember and read this one day? Perhaps, if I send her some posthumous hints and guide her to it.

Her piano playing improves from day to day. She is sight-reading now, I can hear her. Sight-reading! I am so afraid that coming from her it could all mean more complicity. Our old life was so direct, straightforward. It is enough that Clothilde should be thoughtful and considerate.

I am going to die, Joseph, wait for me. You *are* waiting! Open your heart. Don't smile at what I have just written. This is an adventure of the mind.

This notebook will be our masterwork. At the beginning of this year, only a short time before you died, you read an article in a Marxist review by Ernst Mökle. And you summarized it for me. Substantially he was saying that there would always be a sufficient number of creative minds around, in whatever kind of society we have, whether they're to provide for a hundred thousand people, ten thousand or only a thousand. And you added with a smile: 'He forgot about us, we worked for the two of us. That Mökle didn't take his ideas far enough!'

We shall be leaving Copeyne in twenty days, lock, stock and barrel. Sabine maintains that it will take us the summer at least to get settled in Paris! Get settled!

For this notebook the countdown is nearly over. The loop will be looped and it will strangle us. But we shall be reborn! In the days that remain I must try to convey what the Great War meant to us. I shall copy out some of the finest letters our young soldier Martial sent us from the front. But first perhaps I shall copy out one of my own pieces. Forgive me. It has just turned up, written on faded paper probably about the time my daughter Sophie was born. Shortly after, Clothilde had her miscarriage, though the following year she caught up with her sister in what both of them saw as an innocent race for children by having little Pierre. Your son, Pierre! War had just been declared.

Well, perhaps we did get married and produce all this human offspring for fear of growing old together, and because we were afraid we might end by killing each other. Life, yes, but not with wrinkles!

Clothilde has just stopped playing. This evening we are dining at Copeyne. And this will be the first of a long series of farewell dinners. Sabine has sold Copeyne, a house that was never really mine, so deeply have I put my roots down here. Does she realize this? I grew up at Saint-Pardom with you, arm in arm, flesh of your flesh. You don't uproot an oak tree, you chop it into sections like these pages.

In the bowels of the earth the roots search not for black oblivion but for the darkness that gives life.

On our white beach, our bed, in the place that was yours, I shall still talk to you for a few nights more: a sigh, a whistling whisper.

This notebook is like the palm of your hand. And as I place my lips on it, I thank you. For so many pleasures to come!

# 14 April 1913. From me. The Toad

It all started four days ago. Sabine said: 'I won't have that toad in the cellar!' It was more than you could do not to smile, Joseph. Sabine had only just got over the birth of Sophie, my younger child, and there she was back in charge of everything already. 'That toad is dangerous! Toads spit. And burn your skin. And what's it doing in the house anyway at this time of the year?' Clothilde muttered: 'They bring good luck!' Then she laid down her knife and fork, as if she were no longer hungry. Leaning back in her chair and folding her arms over her pregnant belly, she repeated: 'Yes, they bring good luck.' And you stood up, kissed Clothilde on the brow and asked her if she wished to go home. Sabine suggested that Marie stay there with Henri and the baby for the night. What's more she added: 'It would be much simpler if we all lived under the same roof. It's more comfortable here. Saint-Pardom is too big. Noellie's granddaughter has written to me from Tressens. She'd look after all our children!'

In her cradle Sophie started crying. Sabine stood up. 'That child is always starving!' And Sabine walked out in the middle of the meal, proud to be the good mother, breastfeeding her children; whereas Clothilde, if you remember, was unable to feed Marie for more than three or four days. I turned to Clothilde: 'Don't pay any attention. Are you feeling all right?' Clothilde nodded. You sat down again, Joseph, and we carried on with our meal. Clothilde looked at us strangely. You smiled at her: 'Tell us about the toad.' In a soft voice Clothilde explained that a toad always makes its home in a place where something has been lost. She

163

rather made fun of this superstition, but went on all the same: 'It's true, that's what I've been told.' We continued eating. Clothilde sent us a questioning look. We started imagining what kind of things could have been lost, what incidents forgotten, which might justify the presence in my house of this amphibian. But we came to no satisfactory conclusion. Then Clothilde asked me exactly where the toad was. When I told her that he never left the pile of logs in the cellar, she gave a sweet smile with a hint of weariness and, raising both her hands to her bun, she removed the hairpins one by one and let her hair tumble round her, something that her sister forbids her to do as it's hardly correct at mealtimes, and she murmured: 'I feel better like this. And now I understand.' 'What?' 'The toad in the woodpile!' 'Explain!' 'I'll tell you later . . .'

It was when we were in the drawing-room drinking mint tea, you Joseph poking the fire and I with my eye on Clothilde and her swollen belly sitting in an armchair staring at you, that we were granted an explanation. 'It warms the heart, a wood fire, doesn't it? That toad is sitting on a logpile homesick for the kind of warmth that's been forgotten in this house. A lost heart? It sounds silly, but that's what it is.' Then you glanced at me, Joseph, and I lowered my eyes. Clothilde had taken us by surprise. Then she went on, looking at both of us: 'I'm sorry, Roland, I'm sorry, Joseph. Let's not talk about the toad any more, if you don't mind!' Sabine came back to join us, still buttoning her blouse, as if further to aggravate her sister. Silence. Oh, the violence that lay behind those silences! An unhappy quartet! Sabine turned to me: 'This mint tea is far too sweet. And sugar's expensive!' Then after another sip, back to the toad: 'I want to get rid of it tomorrow!'

When the evening was over, Sabine and Clothilde wrapped Marie in a great big shawl, 'for the walk home, to keep her nice and warm'. You came up to me, Joseph, and said, 'You've stopped sending me your poems?' 'So have you,' I answered. Neither of us smiled. 'So you're going on with your notes?' 'So are you,' I answered. And as though you were hoping to break the ice of our fiercely sombre mood with a conciliatory remark, you asked, 'How's Livy getting on?' 'About as well as Virgil!' I answered. And you grabbed hold of my hand and squeezed it hard. Too hard perhaps.

Today I still feel your hand imprinted on mine, the hand with which I am writing this!

For three days I left the cellar door open. Now and then I would go down and talk to the toad. 'Go away,' I would say. 'Hurry up and get out of here! This isn't the right house for you!' Stupid things I said to him, things I really meant which came out without thinking. 'She doesn't want you here! Understand?' But I never went up to him. He would stare at me from the top of the woodpile as I popped in and out, taking care not to come too close to him.

On each of the next three evenings, on our way home from Saint-Pardom where Clothilde in her seventh month of pregnancy was ill in bed, Sabine would ask me: 'You have killed it, haven't you?' And as we walked back side by side, with Henri in my arms and Sophie in hers, I would give no reply. Not to answer is my only hope of defence. Or my only hope of attack. Yesterday she said: 'Very well. I shall do it myself tomorrow morning!'

This morning I went to the cellar very early. Day had only just broken. I sat down on the floor in front of the woodpile. The toad, still on top, gazed at me in astonishment, digging his little claws into a log. Again and again I must have said something like: 'For God's sake make your escape! It's now or never!' But he never budged. So then I stood up and stretched out my hands, determined to take him outside, far away, to the bottom of the garden. At once he spat at them. A burning jet of spittle. I rushed upstairs to the kitchen sink where I splashed water all over my hands and forearms, rubbing myself vigorously. Then I went back to the cellar. The toad was still there at the same spot, looking alarmed. I picked up a piece of wood and struck my first blow

165

with my eyes shut. Then opening them to see that I had missed and that the beast was trying to creep between the logs, I struck again, this time with my eyes open, and saw that the toad was crushed and dying. I attacked him furiously, for the head was still there, the eyes staring at me. It was all over! So with two sticks I picked the little body up and, holding my arms out in front of me, emerged from the cellar only to see, Joseph, distraught, pale and out of breath, suddenly dashing up to stammer out the news, almost sobbing: 'Clo has lost our child.'

I dropped the sticks and the toad. I wanted to make some gesture towards you, but you moved away. Sabine called me from the house. You looked at me and said: 'You tell her. That's your job.' And you left.

I walked straight up to my study, meeting Sabine on the stairs. I simply muttered: 'Clothilde has lost her child,' without even noticing the expression on her face at the news.

And here I have been for hours and hours, brandishing this fountain pen as one might a stick of wood, furiously attacking a ridiculous victim with staring eyes. Astonished that this little murder should seem more serious to me than the death of a child.

You came back during the afternoon to tell me that Clothilde was asleep and there was nothing to worry about. And then standing behind me, where still at my desk I had not moved when you entered, you slipped your fingers round the back of my neck and whispered: 'I'm sorry about this morning, but you frightened me. Why did you have to kill that toad?'

I know that these little incidents happen in life. But on my right wrist there is a kind of imprint and there are burns on my forearms, all sorts of little surface marks that mask an even deeper wound. We too have spat in each other's faces, Joseph, you and I. With our eyes wide open. You and I as well.

For a long time you held me by the neck. I had to struggle to my feet to shake off your grip. And then, face to face with you – I don't know which one of us first leant towards the other, first drew the other to him – we kissed with closed mouths, crushing our lips till they were forced apart and the ramparts of our teeth ground together. And we never even grasped each other's hands. Like flying buttresses, each needed to uphold the other in order to remain erect. We shall never reach a final definition of ourselves.

Then you stepped back, breathing heavily, and clenching your left hand you banged your fist into your right-hand palm and said briskly: 'I love Clo, you know! There's nothing to worry about! We will have our son!' And with a smile you went on: 'She's promised me that already.' The high-pitched 'already' had an almost joyful note about it.

You returned to Clothilde. We are keeping Marie here with Henri and Sophie. Sabine has decided to send for Noellie's granddaughter. She arrives tomorrow. Soon we shall all be living here together at Copeyne. Saint-Pardom will become 'our place' again.

I have just glanced through one of last month's magazines which I picked up by chance, and there I noticed a highly significant photograph of young French scouts on manoeuvres in the Clamart woods. And underneath it a statement made by a certain Vice-Admiral Besson: 'These military exercises demonstrate the ingenuity and first-rate training of our future combat troops.' So they all want to go to war? Let them fight! All those children were the same age as Martial! Hurry up, Joseph, and have your son. If war is declared, *we* will not fight it. Their return match has nothing to do with the offensive we are launching! This second slope of our life is a downward one, but we still have to live it!

I am going to pick up the sticks in front of the cellar door and throw the toad out in true Bérard fashion. After that I shall go and light a big log fire in the drawing-room. To warm myself up. It's almost as if we were already under the same roof, isn't it? Buttressing each other up. Something else for us to share. Mouths shut.

You see, I am still writing my notes. I shall go on with them. And Martial is still here, insinuating himself. Hard as I try to knock him out, each time I miss him.

# Three letters from Martial

Villeneuve, 3 November 1914

Hallo Joseph, hallo Roland,
Yes, it's Martial! I miss you. I know you think about me. This letter will come as a pleasant surprise to you, because it's sent from Villeneuve while you imagine me to be a hundred leagues from here. Here I am, in fact, still at Villeneuve, and I can't tell you when I'm leaving. If I go with the 1914 call-up, under special dispensation as I'm the youngest, then it would be between the lst and the 6th of November, otherwise I'll have to leave later.

Whatever happens, if it's not too much trouble, could you send me a small parcel with three pairs of woollen socks? It's an easy parcel to make up and it would be hard for me to find anything as good. I'll buy everything else myself. I need a pair of gloves, an oilskin to protect me from the rain and some sort of hood to stop the water running down the back of my neck.

I'm in very good health and I'd like to know if anything has changed for you. Couldn't you write to me? My comrades sometimes ask me whether I have any parents. If you knew how nice it was to receive a little word from home, even just a brief note now and then, though long letters are best. Just a little news about my home town and the country round, to know whether any of my old friends have been killed or wounded.

It's been raining here every day. How are they managing at La

Sarriete to get the sowing done? I wish I could put my hand to a harrow or a plough! Ever since I got to Villeneuve, you know, I've been playing soldiers on the main square every day.

Anyway, let's hope I'll be home for the harvest, if I can't do the sowing. I'll enjoy that.

It's not that I'm down in the dumps, but there are lots of things I like better and I miss them. Peaceful evenings on the farm, for example, going to market, the Lion d'Or café, the shooting-parties, the local ball where I could watch and learn how to dance, and all those fields I so enjoyed looking after. Let's hope these happy days won't be taken from us for ever and the day isn't too far off when I'll be able to tease Old Adeline again. Does she still sing out of tune?

I say, you two! You first put the idea of travel in my mind. My wishes would come true, wouldn't they, if they ever got round to sending me to Turkey! But I don't suppose they will. I expect they'd rather send me to some sector of the Front in search of glory, if not death! But I don't mind telling you I'll do my best to hang on to this bag of bones and defend it to the bitter end. Let's change the subject and think of nicer things. That's what I tell myself every day. It's in my nature and you should do the same. That's my advice to you. It's the best way to be happy in this life. Go to La Sarriete in good heart and give that message to them. They're like the earth, those two, they don't need to read. Your going there will prove that! They'll be reading *you*.

How are you and everyone else? Tell me how you and all our friends are getting on. And your good ladies and their children. The war's all for them, you know! Surrelac's son is going to the Front, isn't he?

Well, time is getting short and I must bring this letter to a close! Say hallo to everyone for me, all my friends and relations, and the town too when you're passing. And don't forget the big elm tree, you know the one I mean on the way to La Sarriete? Fondest love and kisses from your son, to all of you,

Martial.

PS Give my greetings as well to the folks at Polignac, Marsolan and Tressens. I'm enclosing a photograph. Quite the young warrior, your Martial, isn't he?

Ville-sous-Bois, 29 March 1915

Dear friends!
I'm not too sure what to do, and as it's nearly April Fool's Day I thought I'd send you a little *poisson d'avril* together with a few things I picked up in the woods of Hesse just beyond this village of wooden huts where we spend our rest-days. I won't tell you that I fished my *poisson* in the Meuse (the river, not the Department), because you'd never believe me. And you won't believe either that the little sisters of the flowers accompanying this letter are at this very hour, 8.30 in the evening, all covered in snow. But it will have gone by tomorrow morning, for the weather is set fair and the winter is over, well and truly over.

These little flowers will help you understand how pretty the woods must look in the spring, when people feel happy. There are blackbirds too. They sing just like ours and look the same too. Now and again we eat a few, but with a Lebel rifle you have to take careful aim. It's different with the hares and the wild boar. We shoot to order, a whole platoon of us, if need be. The other day a boar gave us quite a turn. The Boche must have been firing at it too, because it came crashing along at top speed towards our trench. We thought it was the Boche rattling our barbed wire. The sentries opened fire. We dashed to our loopholes and soon realized it was only a boring old boar that had had the bad luck to get itself tangled up. I need hardly tell you it had ten bullets in it.

Now that's something you didn't know, isn't it, all you folks?

We're not just after the Boche! There's time to go shooting at other things too.

Good news at camp for the 2nd Battalion. Our General came to say hallo. In the afternoon the terribletorials joined up with us to launch an attack on a barrel of wine which the General had treated us to. But we also suffered an unfortunate setback. Taking full advantage of the fog, a horde of fleas concentrated massive forces in the shirt of my pal, Antoine – you remember him, he's from Montestruc – and laid siege to him on every side. The battle is still raging now, while I'm writing.

But I must stop or I shall run out of paper. Don't be too worried about me. Here at camp, you know, we have a sing-song every evening. The only thing missing is petticoat! The other day someone spotted a woman at the crossroads. At least fifty chaps rushed to get a look at her. A sight for sore eyes, just imagine! I embrace you.

Your ever-loving Martial.

PS Just enough space for a couple more words and then no more paper. Did you receive the Boche cartoons I sent you? According to them, there's a big naval battle going on in the woods at Polignac! Perhaps you've seen their torpedo boats passing through La Sarriete? Hugs and kisses to my folks at home! Tell them to keep their eyes open!

The trenches, 27 May 1916

Hallo, my two friends!
Yesterday I received both your letters at once, the one dated the 13th, which was overdue, and the one my father dictated to you on the 15th. By the way, I must tell you how grateful I am. I'll never be able to repay you for all your kindness, and I hope they do the best they can for you at La Sarriete.

My father makes my mouth water when he says the partridges are

172

coming to feed with the hens. And it amused me to hear that he's working so hard he's not sure whether he's going to bed or getting up, and that when he gets dressed his breeches are still warm. I haven't stopped laughing yet! Please tell him I'm short of envelopes, so I won't write him a separate letter. Did he receive my last three postal orders?

Please read this to my mother: I really admire you, mother dear, the way you keep your courage up in spite of everything. I was afraid you might lose heart and I'm so pleased you have such strength of mind and endurance. Have a good cry when Joseph and Roland are there, it'll do you a power of good. You talk about the high jinks we'll have when I get home with all this money. The day I get wed I bet I'll see you waltzing around like a mad thing with all our guests. The thought of a family gathering makes me want to get you drunk as a donkey. That's for her.

Now the war is dragging on I can see it's my duty to amuse the older ones, the married men, and do as much as I can to help them take their minds off the stresses and strains they're under. It's natural that it's far worse for them than for us bachelors. So please try and send me, one by one and in the following order, this little list of song-sheets. Here are the titles: 1) 'It's just the thing', 2) 'A man and his breeks', 3) 'Water at tuppence a glass'. This way I can enlarge my repertoire. I've tried hard to think up a few songs of my own, but I'm not much good at it. With this letter I'm enclosing the last one I composed. It's far from perfect but it went down extremely well.

Do as I do, try not to let things upset you. Then you'll see. With patience we'll get through this time of cruelty and suffering. We have all been too happy-go-lucky: let us forget and not forget. Have you still as much work to do at the Town Hall?

Caresses to you both and to you all, all of you, and please stroke my sisters' hair for me. I want them to prepare for my wedding!
                                                                    Martial.

PS Antoine insists on knowing whether you've been to Montestruc. Have you seen Hélène? She must be a beauty for Antoine to be so stuck on this idea of his. How has she taken the death of her man? After all, you were at the wedding. It's up to you to make a trip there. Antoine wants to know. It's just for him. I'll pass it on.

# Twenty-seventh day

The pages of this notebook cut me like blades of grass. This paper world, which still makes everything possible, is rejecting me already. Today, 8 June 1935, barely a month after you died, Joseph, I can see quite clearly, thanks to this ink and this fountain pen which I wield as we once wielded each other, that our life is bound up with words and that if we accuse them of taking over our life it may be only because of our desire to play a double game. What if we were going to live our life twice over after all? Two portraits of us. The one engraved out of our living struggle for existence. The other inscribed in the upstrokes and downstrokes of this notebook. Is this being sacrilegious? Does this second life cancel out the first? Or is it a springboard?

This notebook, newborn, is growing away from me. When are you coming to see me? When shall I see you again? One life is ending, another beginning. The gap between them will have lasted only a few days. A slight breach, that's all. I shall close this notebook and cling to it, straining my fingers and my hands to withstand the oncoming wind which threatens to close the double doors of that great gateway, the rainbow. The water of a little brook is already turning red with our blood, as it does the day the butcher slaughters his beasts. A donkey, a cat, a toad, a wild boar, all the murders in this notebook are a prelude to our death! We have sharpened our claws on our love, till we have worn the skin away. And here we are, flayed alive, ready to be reborn. Oh, the vanity of all hope devoid of hopelessness. How much time does one need to take one's bearings? A whole lifetime? Nothing ever gets really settled.

The day he returned, soon after the Armistice, Martial took us down a peg. Emphasizing his sing-song voice he said to us in front of his parents: 'Oh shut up, the two of you! I'm the ex-service-man, you two are ex-noncombatants!' Yes, we lived that war in a funk-hole, dealing with problems at the Town Hall, busy registering births, deaths and marriages. You, Joseph, even entered the birth of your own son Pierre yourself, after taking over from a brave penpusher who had gone off to fight. But what was the bravery for? Revenge and destruction? This war has left me nothing but a smell in my nostrils: the stink of civil-service paper. And I owe this shared memory to you, Joseph, thanks to your acute sense of smell.

The Armistice was a celebration for everyone except us. People began to point a finger at us: 'They didn't fight in the war!' And we stuck to our municipal duties right to the bitter end. Until the war memorial had been erected on the promenade and the list of names it had taken us years to compile had been chiselled in the stone. All those names. Other people's lives. Other people's loves.

Even Sabine and Clothilde looked forward to us leaving them to spend the day together. Saint-Pardom became our refuge again, not unlike a jail. And we pretended each of us to be passionately involved in our respective fields of study, while our only desire was to return to a past of actions and gestures that bound us together, still drawing us on and trying to drag us with it. Towards what? Sometimes we questioned each other with a furtive look. But our ageing flesh was a barrier that forbade effusion. We would let it rest with that buttressed kiss the day of the toad, which was also the day of a stillborn child, a day of wastage and loss. And when at times one of us started a phrase beginning, 'You remember . . .', we would halt it there. And no sooner had a smile flickered over our lips than we turned our eyes away. Only now and then would I take your hand or you take mine, and for a brief moment a squeeze of the fingers would be enough to quieten us and encourage us to be still, when the disorder in our bodies was still clamouring.

Then we went back to writing poems, so much dead skin that we never even bothered to exchange them. All I remember is one rough draft on a page you forgot to tear up. I found it when emptying the basket on your desk and on it you had written an unfinished poem, already crossed out:

> ~~The sky has been shipwrecked~~
> ~~And against its upturned hull~~
> ~~We have beaten our fists~~
> ~~Till they bled~~ . . .

Obviously it was a bad start. Shipwrecked, bled! But any poem that's worth its salt had one false start. We never knew how to match our words to our embraces, that is all. We loved one another. Nothing crazy about that. It just *is*. Or perhaps we went too far in what we did, into a realm where language of any kind becomes superfluous. Oh yes, our great masterwork is our life! These notes only touch the surface of it and with us it will be obliterated.

The day before his wedding Martial had turned up to ask for a suit to wear. The same suit he was wearing twenty-seven days ago when they buried you next to your mother, or rather when they were laying your coffin next to the coffin of Mademoiselle Terrefort, unmarried mother. Put on the shelf as if in an underground Bazaar! I know they won't care what they do with *me*, the son of a Cayenne convict!

That day, with no sense of shame, Martial tried his suit on in front of us. Stark naked for a moment, he turned to face us. And he laughed: 'I've got plenty of hair now! I'm a soldier, a real *poilu*!' We were in the bedroom, the very place where he had his first orgasm. Our little rogue.

And as I walked him back to the gates he remarked what a disgrace it was that the land at Polignac had been lying fallow for more than thirty years. And I just added: 'She's yours.' Yes, the way I referred to it then, it might have been another wife for him to take. He grinned happily and simply said: 'You really ought to thank *me*. I'm going to wake the sleeping beauty and bring her back to life!'

And so it came about, Joseph, that Sabine was surprised to see her tenant-farmer at your funeral. Twenty-seven days ago. Twenty-seven days! She has sold Copeyne, but I'll do all I can to ensure that Polignac stays with its lord and master. Our lord and master, Martial! How the memory of our eager flesh stretches and strains, still haunting us.

This morning Martial sent me his younger son, Martin, now twelve, with a basketful of peaches and apricots and a brief note: 'Dear Roland. Empty this basket, it's for you and Joseph's wife. Send the basket back with my son! I told him to knock before he went in. I love you, old man. I hear you are going away. Your good lady came and told me. I sent her packing. Polignac is mine to make love to! At least come and see me before you leave. Your part of a son, Martial.'

Your part of a son? Young Martin took to his heels. He was very scared. Clothilde offered him a franc which he refused.

# The last day. Eve of departure

It is fulfilment, incompletion that forges the strongest of bonds. I offer you this thought, Joseph, as a token of tenderness and good sense, for good sense is the most brutal of all truth.

For three weeks I have shut myself away in this study, labelling files, classifying papers and letters, discovering all sorts of notes in your handwriting and mine which could have furnished a more comprehensive and spectacular work. But all that really matters is the passion and desperation of our struggle not to find fulfilment in each other in order to draw even closer together.

There are no fixed rules to govern the life of a genuine couple. There is no way of codifying or reconstituting their sparring or their congress, their gestures, glances or desires, when these are doomed to be insatiable.

The strongest of bonds depends upon place as well. This town was our guardian and its horizons were our temptation.

So I could see no point in reproducing here all those notes we took during our numerous winter journeys, from 1921 to the one in January this year, 1935, when we had to make a sudden exodus from the port of Alexandria because of anxiety about your health. Winters abroad and summers here! Home in the summer to find our children taller and our wives in competition, matching ambition on the one side against discretion on the other. And the winter, all those winters, discovering Crete, the Nubians and the

Nile, Ephesus and even Kabul. I nearly succumbed to temptation and rescued at least one page from that travel diary in which you recounted your impressions of our visit to the Red City, the forbidden City of Genghis Khan. But just as I was about to do so, something told me to beware, as if all these notes written so long ago were in rebellion, warning me. The greatest journey of our lives was the one our bodies made, a voyage of discovery with explorations inland.

And the day you died, when Clothilde came to ask me to prepare you for what would be your final journey, then too I admit I was afraid. I would have given anything to say no. But she had such a set look in her eyes that I had to agree. And I must confess that the moment I first opened this notebook, the idea of withholding this scene until the end had already taken root. As a kind of moral?

On the floor at the foot of the bed, on the very spot where we had spreadeagled Martial, Clothilde laid some large bathtowels out. Then I picked you up in my arms. You were heavy, such a heavy weight. I lowered you down. Round your body Clothilde placed several large jugs of clean water and some basins for dirty water and, handing me a sponge, simply murmured: 'You'll have to do it.' She was in tears.

Then I took some scissors and starting from the bottom cut your nightgown open. I laid each half back on either side of you, to reveal a body strange to me, pale, tired, emaciated, with your bone structure outlined through the skin, like the ridges of rocks and reefs just under the surface. Then, before I could get really started, I had to cut round the armholes, slide the two tubes of cloth off your arms, and pull out from under your body what was left of the garment, your first shroud. Behind me, Clothilde was on her knees watching me work without looking at you any more. I washed you, your face first, very gently, sponging your nose, your chin and your neck, then the arms, the armpits, your chest and your hollow stomach. It was then, I think, that everything misted over. Was that sobbing mine or Clothilde's? I rolled you over on the towels and then, again and again, as I squeezed out the sponge dipped in clean water, came that curious to and fro, far too frequent, from your body to the jug, while I slowly washed your back. My last official rites. That is all I wish to say. I simply have to set down that I did it. One question remains to be answered: how do we become so disfigured, so worn, gaunt and wrinkled? Should I have been humbled by it?

What is left is the body of this text, the skin of this notebook, these fragments like chosen extracts from our favourite classics, but selected at random by the heart, not analytically. It may not quite be poetry, but it is all that remains: our progress together through these pages.

I shall leave for Paris alone. Tomorrow. Alone with Sabine! One can live with solitude but not with isolation. With her, and my son, I shall be isolated. Confirming their triumph and my damnation.

And up there the shock I have suffered will remain anonymous. I shall cry your name everywhere, at every chance encounter, whereas here, where we were always so strong to govern our emotions, I dare not do it.

Should I also have included that long piece you wrote in August 1928, to welcome the return of the lone sailor, Alain Gerbault? You called it *Our trip round the world*. And from here in Saint-Pardom you opened up the furthest corners of the earth, describing each subtle scent, the faintest creak of a sail. In that text you call me *Firecrest*. Thus each of us is the vessel for the other, his adventurer. Love always leaves its wake behind.

Should I also have copied out those press-cuttings recounting the sordid murder of Hélène and her three children at Montestruc by her second husband, Antoine, the Great War hero? Now what year was that?

Bounding, binding us, one place unites us still. For the first time since you died Clothilde has gone to close the gates of Saint-Pardom. This evening we shall take our last meal together. I shall not sleep here again, for tomorrow we leave at dawn. And when on the road to Cazauban I greet the rising sun, it is you I shall be welcoming.

I saw Martial once again. Not at Polignac. At the lawyer's. I made him a gift of this land. Sabine came with me. But she said nothing. She clutched her handbag, her little booted feet drawn back under her chair, continually crossing and recrossing them as though she expected to tip forward in fury. And Martial, sitting bolt upright with his hands on his knees, said nothing either. When it had all been signed and we were parting company, Sabine ignored him. I went up to him, kissed him on the forehead and gave him my thanks.

A lifetime of thanks from us. Everything starts again. How good it is to die with you, Joseph. Fertile land. Martial, Martin, and all the rest to come! One day perhaps they too will read in this notebook the ever-living present. Farewell, Joseph, now I am closing it as I once closed your pencil-case.

# An additional note.
## Two letters discovered in the Notebook

Paris
7 February 1936

My dearest sister,
I have waited four days before sending you this news. Your
brother-in-law, Roland, died during the night of the 1st and 2nd
of February. He was found stabbed at first light in a bush not far
from the Château de Vincennes, close to the barracks of the same
name. Henri went to the morgue to identify his father. As the
police decided against an investigation the body was returned to
us yesterday. And to take the simplest solution, Sophie, Henri and
I opted for a common graveyard.

I am asking you to notify the Town Hall. You will find the
necessary documents enclosed. The mention 'accidental death'
shows in itself that there is no need for you to broadcast the facts
behind this little drama. Since we came here, Roland has spoken
very little to us, and he went out a great deal, especially at night.

Among his papers I found this envelope, addressed to you, which
appears to contain a key. I hope it's something you've been
looking for.

We should like to come and spend next summer with you. I have
always loved Saint-Pardom. Can you take us? With your own
children there we could all be together again! I await your answer,
but please, no commiseration. It all happened so quickly, we have

hardly had time to feel any pain. As for our poor Roland, according to the forensic surgeon he received the first blow in the abdomen. Apparently he didn't suffer. And that's the main thing. Life here in Paris at the start of this year seems full of disturbances. Protest marches of every kind . . . Henri thinks this is the end of an era. I am sending you a photograph of Roland. The only one I ever had really. From now on the proper place for it is in that study.

I look forward to hearing from you shortly, sister dear. As soon as we can, let us leave these painful memories behind us. Your loving elder sister, Sabine.

Saint-Pardom, the eve of my departure.

My Clo,
With this letter I am enclosing the key to the top drawer of the desk. There you will find a notebook which I have just locked away and in which I have noted down all those things which Joseph and I stole from one another and later concealed from you. Turn the pages of this notebook as if you were throwing the shutters of Saint-Pardom open to the sunshine and the wind. Do not judge us. Share with us. Tender kisses. Farewell, Roland.

A notebook in a locked drawer. Violation, both the adventure and the text. I entreat you. Please.